HELL'S BROOD:
VOLUME I

AN EVE OF LIGHT STORY COLLECTION

HARAMBEE K. GREY-SUN

HYPERVERSE BOOKS, LLC

Cover design by The Cover Collection.

Print ISBN-13: 978-1-64044-000-5

Ebook ISBN-13: 978-1-64044-001-2

Published by **HyperVerse Books, LLC**

www.hyperversebooks.com

Crossing genres without apologies.

CONTENTS

The Lark   1

Heaven's Gun   22

FoolKillers   56

Knotty & Ice   82

Rogue Beauty   116

About the Author   165

About the Series   167

Also by Harambee K. Grey-Sun   169

THE LARK

The plane landed around 11:50 pm. Danny had been promised the car rental booth would close at 12:30 am. She ran through the little two-story airport as fast as her legs could carry her, all 145 pounds of her and her duffle bag, down a frozen escalator and through an automatic door that refused to open automatically. She reached the rental desk at 11:59.

Closed.

Fantastic.

She'd come all the way from Houston to Who-the-Hell-Cared-Where, Pennsylvania to meet up with some no-names who'd posted a classified for singer who had a unique voice and was willing to travel off the beaten path. This was not a promising start.

It was the middle of wherever, but the gig promised to pay quite well—better than a weekend spent bartending, anyway. And the man on the other side of the phone had sounded sincere. But near-desperation could filter all sorts of sounds one didn't want to hear on a cell phone—static, background traffic, snickering . . .

The airport had damn near been sucked dry of sound. Behind her, the luggage turnstile crept with a scratchy whisper as her fellow passengers silently retrieved their bags. She trudged over and eased herself onto a bench, watching for her two bags but more closely observing the twelve, sizing them up, wondering about the type of folks who would come to such an area.

Surely none of them were here on business—though one had claimed otherwise. He'd tried to make conversation with her on the plane, insisting her was a producer coming out this way to look for "lost-and-unfound" talent because he'd heard rumors . . . She thought it curious anyone would come out this way looking for any kind of talent, and she quickly grew suspicious when she realized the guy only introduced himself as being in the music biz after she'd introduced herself as a singer. She'd tuned the guy out for the remainder of the trip.

Presently, she got a better look at him and the others. Even late-night travelers didn't dress in such a patchwork fashion. Many of their shirts seemed to be flannel, but none featured a single distinct color she could name. Their slacks looked like paper bags sewn together, and their shoes didn't appear practical for anything other than standing still. Through lazy lids, the more she regarded them and their sullen expressions, the less they appeared human to her. They were more like rejects from something—products of a broken mold, still unwisely being used. But that was just exhaustion blowing nonsense into her head. Exhaustion and frustration.

This was her first time traveling outside of the southwest. Even at the ripe old age of thirty-two, there was so much she didn't know about the various cultures existing inside the Brave Not-So-New World of the United States. But she was intelligent enough to know, if not always acknowledge, that each region had its own style. Perfectly normal within a limited radius.

She leaned back and allowed her eyelids to relax completely. This was going to be her first important gig in months, and she probably wouldn't be in any shape to perform. Not on just a few hours of sleep. What was she thinking agreeing to do a breakfast performance, singing in the background at some gathering of farmers, a gathering where the audience would surely be more engrossed in their biscuits and gravy than her voice? Yeah, she was thinking of rent money—but what were the possibilities for any meaningful exposure? The guy who'd auditioned her over the phone just two days prior claimed she was exactly what they needed—a Tex-Mex songstress with a voice more rasp than honey—and he seemed happy enough to send her a plane ticket. At that point, she wasn't going to argue about the arrival time, nor think twice about the two layovers she would have to endure before getting here.

Her eyelids fluttered open, piqued by the realization of complete silence. The turnstile had stopped turning. The claim area was empty. And there was no sign of any abandoned luggage. She stood, glumly looking all about her. *Great.* On top of everything else, she'd a lost bag. And, of course, the service office was closed, its workers undoubtedly as long gone as the car rental folks. Luckily, if not happily, she'd packed all her essentials in her clunky carryon. Deodorant, comb, clean undergarments . . . She hoped the breakfast audience would be more concerned about the appearance of their eggs and flapjacks than of her.

No sense in speculating. Her immediate worry was finding a place to lay her head, preferably near a source of clean water she could use to freshen up afterward, even if she only had time to splash it on her face and pits. Empty or not, she was in an airport. There had to be at least one hotel within walking distance, even in a weird country town.

She exited through the glass doors and crossed the pickup lane. There was nothing beyond the parking lot. No sign of a hotel, motel, or even a shack promising a cheap bed and breakfast. Nothing but darkness and some darker hint of trees far on the horizon.

The parking lot was just as vacant. Her fellow passengers' rides must've arrived before the plane landed, ready to pick up as soon as they exited the building. Final landing of the day, the airport staff had all apparently taken off as well.

Well, maybe not all of them . . . She spotted a white van in the farthest corner of the lot. Bright white, as if it were covered in a layer of fresh snow. Its windows were as black as a snowman's coal eyes. The impression of snow in the middle of June . . . Something was off, and she trusted her intuition.

Someone was still around, maybe close by. Maybe in the vehicle, preparing to start it up, ready to leave. But there'd be no approaching the vehicle, asking for a lift. She knew her horror movie scenarios. She backed up a few steps before doing a one-eighty back through the glass doors. Best to stay in a well-lit building.

She snatched up a map as she passed by the car rental desk, wondering just why all of the airport's lights were still on and all the doors unlocked, as if it were just past noon rather than just past midnight.

She picked up the desk's blue phone while gazing at the cab advertisements on the back of the folded map. No dial tone. She figured it was too much to ask that everything be working at this hour. Anyway, calling at this point seemed far more trouble than it was worth: Trying to stay awake while the cab arrived, then trusting it to take her to a decent motel without running up the meter . . . She'd have been more inclined if she could trust her smartphone to stay up with her through all that, but she'd realized when boarding the plane that her phone was almost out of juice. Turning it on now and keeping it on until the cab arrived would kill it. Of course, she'd had the brilliant foresight to pack the charger with the other nonessentials in her lost luggage.

She left the desk, unfolding the map as she wandered. It seemed she hadn't been too far off considering this area the middle of wherever. The map showed only the airport at its center with nothing but an open field surrounding it. At the far edges were the trees she thought she'd made out in the dark. The map had no scale or anything else useful to determine the distance from the airport to the trees. It didn't matter to her. In the morning, she'd be driving through it, not walking it—even if the map oddly showed no roads or paths.

She looked up from the map and spotted a ladies' room. No sense in waiting till sunrise to wash travel's grime off her face. Something also had to be done with what was left of her late-night burger and fries. She checked three stalls before finding one with toilet paper, hung her bag on the door's hook, and then sat down with a sigh.

She'd get some shuteye on the bench in the baggage claim area. It was barely even comfortable to sit on, but when the car rental desk opened at six, she'd be in a prime position to get what she needed and get the hell out of there. Her performance started at eight; the location she'd been given surely couldn't be that far away.

She sighed again as she wiped and pulled up her jeans. She'd a funny feeling in her stomach. It never failed. Dropping a little load always made her a little hungry. During her earlier mad dash, she'd noticed a vending machine upstairs, one containing nuts and dried fruit in addition to the usual cavity creators; she'd swing by on her way to the bench. She flushed, grabbed her bag, and opened the stall door.

A man stood mere feet away, staring back at her.

Her shriek created some distance, as if her voice had arms that shoved him back a few feet while also causing her to stumble backward. She caught herself before falling onto the toilet.

Whatever had caused him to retreat a few steps, the grizzled man appeared in no way frightened. He wore a stained, gray jumpsuit and tattered ball cap; his eyes were bloodshot and his hands were scarred many times over. He'd clearly experienced plenty of frightening things in his time. His sun-ravaged skin gave her the impression of vet from a long ago war, or maybe a long one still going.

"Ex-excuse me." She wanted to rush past him, but she lacked the energy for such a burst. Fear didn't jolt her; it nearly paralyzed her.

The man said nothing as the right side of his upper lip curled —a wavering snarl probably deciding whether to growl or curse at her.

She couldn't run, but she could talk. "Ar-are you lost?" She could ask stupid questions. Of course the old creep didn't belong in the ladies' room.

The man didn't take his eyes off her, and didn't stop snarling, as he reached into his back pocket.

Danny edged forward out of the stall, now ready to attempt to bolt if this crazy pulled out a knife. Fear was being eclipsed by a need to survive.

The man had no blade, at least not one that he flashed, but an orange badge. He held it up, stomach high. Danny glanced down and saw his picture, a name she couldn't pronounce, and a word she could. *Maintenance.*

Of course. The janitor. That had to be his van outside.

She nodded—almost bowed—and forced a wry smile. "Sorry. I'll get out of your way."

The man didn't move as she stepped toward the exit. He only turned his head, letting his eyes follow her out.

She breathed relief upon reaching the hall, as if someone who'd been holding a pillow on her face for a full minute had finally let go. She hurried on in some direction, just away from the bathroom, shoving herself through the dead automatic door, casting glances over her shoulders all the while until she was confident the man wasn't creeping after her.

She almost tripped on the first step of the escalator. Catching herself, she tried to regain her breath as she took one last good look behind her.

Still no sign of a pursuer. Also no sign of any cleaning supplies.

Shit.

Exiting the bathroom, she saw no cart with janitorial equipment, no mop-and-bucket, not even so much as a broom or dustpan. Her heart rate increased as her breathing again got away from her. Those meditation classes she'd taken last fall hadn't done much good; she could rarely control her breath when it mattered most. Out-of-control breathing led to out-of-control thinking.

After a few panicking minutes, she managed to consider that "maintenance" didn't necessarily mean "janitor." Maybe the guy was in there to fix something—a clogged sink, perhaps. She hadn't gotten the chance to use one, never even glanced toward the row of sinks after she'd flushed. Maybe his tools had been there.

She walked up the escalator, motivated not by a fear satiated, but by a hunger that had yet to be. She started toward the area where she remembered seeing the vending machines when something caught her eye that she hadn't noticed before: Three small kiosks that—during normal business hours—sold cookies, pretzels, and cheap trinkets, respectively.

As she stared, the odors of chocolate and peanut butter quickened her. She wasn't on a diet—what did she need with nuts or dried fruit from a vending machine? A packaged candy bar that may've been sitting in the machine for six months was easy to resist, but one-day-old or even two-day-old cookies would take a will stronger than a mortal woman's.

But she surprised herself. She wasn't completely at the mercy of the butterflying pangs in her stomach. Eying the kiosks, she convinced herself that she'd easier tolerate a pretzel than one or two cookies. She could never enjoy cookies without milk; the water fountain would do for a salty pretzel. Anyway, the cookies were more heavily guarded.

All three kiosks were in cages, but the cages were loose and flimsy. With enough strength and effort, she could pry one open enough to wedge herself inside. When she checked the cage for the pretzel stand, however, it slid right open. The lock wasn't loose. It had been broken.

She slid on through and put her hands on the glass counter, preparing to hoist herself over. Then she heard it.

It sounded almost like a squeak—two of them. It wasn't her hands. She froze, concentrating on any sound entering her ears. She heard *chittering*. It was coming from behind the counter.

She peered over. Huddled in a ball and staring back at her was a skinny, ill-clad teenage girl. She was clearly trying to make herself as small as possible, like a frightened cat, but she made no attempt to cover her head or shut her wide-open eyes when Danny spotted her.

Those eyes . . . They seemed all pupil, covered with a thin, bluish translucent film. Some kind of disorder—was the girl blind?

"What are you doing?" Danny asked.

The girl said nothing, only stared.

Danny began again: "Are you—?"

The girl interrupted. "Help. Me. Serve. Hive. Them."

The girl physically appeared to be at least sixteen years old, but she spoke with the voice of someone at least half that age, and with a manner of someone plagued with hiccups. Mentally *and* physically disabled. She appeared malnourished and wore ill-fitting clothes and a few of the trinkets from the adjacent kiosk. Her face was smudged and her mousy brown hair looked like a real mouse had run through it. There were dark spots under her eyes—*Those eyes . . .*

"Who are you hiding from?" Danny whispered. "Who's after you?"

"Know. One," the girl said.

No one? "But you just—" Danny stopped herself. The girl

clearly wasn't right in the head, but she was lost, or abandoned. Possibly a runaway. Whichever, she needed help only someone answering 911 could provide.

Danny heaved herself over the counter and crouched, leaning closer to the girl. "I'm going to call for help, okay?" She turned on her cell phone. "You'll be safe soon." No signal. *Damn.* "We're going to have to get from out of here." She began to stand when the girl grabbed at her sleeve.

"Knot. Time."

"What? We have to get the *police* out here." Danny glanced at her phone. "We have to—" She stopped and stared at her phone. The display read 3:55 am.

She hadn't been in the airport for more than thirty minutes, forty-five at most. Was her phone broken, picking up a weird signal? Or had she actually fallen asleep in the baggage claim?

She crouched down again. "Listen. My phone is on its last legs, and I can't get a good signal in here. We have to go outside. I need to get you some proper help."

"Knot. Time. Sun. Wait."

The girl clearly wasn't in full grasp of her situation, and Danny couldn't think of a way to convince her. The fact she was a teenager was bad enough—since hitting her late twenties, Danny had always had a problem relating to anyone not old enough to legally drink—but the fact that the girl's mind was much younger than her body made it even worse. Danny had no kids of her own, and wouldn't know what to do with them if she had, just like she didn't know what to do now. Should she leave the kid here, go outside to make the call, and then return?

She stood up. She needed to get the circulation going in her legs. While stretching, she looked around for the nearest exit—instead, she saw a figure cresting the escalator. The maintenance man.

She shook her head, quietly cursing herself for not thinking of it immediately. The girl was hiding from the old man. She may've been his daughter, she may've been a kidnap victim. At the moment, it didn't matter. Danny had only two thoughts: the old bastard was the abusive sort and the girl had to be kept away from him at all costs.

The man stopped when he stepped on the floor, and made eye contact.

"C'mon!" Danny grabbed the girl by the elbow; she pulled her up with such ease it was as if she didn't even have bones.

She tugged the girl along as she slid out of the cage and headed in the opposite direction from the man who, as far as Danny could tell, wasn't hurrying after them. That was fortunate. With both duffel bag and girl in tow, she couldn't do much more than trot like a crippled dog.

They had to get downstairs. The only working exit she knew was downstairs. And the only stairs she knew were the escalators. The door by which she entered after deplaning would of course be locked, but a frantic mind pushed her in that direction anyway as she kept an eye out for any emergency exits.

After deplaning on the runway, she and the other passengers had to climb a metal staircase and enter the airport on the upper level, where all the terminals were. The blue door, as she suspected, was now locked, as were the blue doors in the other four terminals she checked. The old man hadn't caught up to them—at least Danny didn't hear or see him—but she still felt trapped. She'd seen no red signs, no emergency exits. They'd have to make their way back toward the escalator, back toward him.

"You? Range? El?"

They were the first words the girl had spoken since they'd left the kiosk, and they were even more puzzling than her previous words.

"No," was all Danny could think to say, as she turned on her phone. She hoped to get a signal near the windows. She wasn't quite sure what the girl was asking, but she figured she had an answer as good as any. "My name's Danny."

"Like? Me? Speh? Shell?"

Poor thing. The girl was special all right, but Danny wondered what made her think there was a connection between them. Her phone showed no signal; it only displayed the time. 4:15 am. "I'm nothing special," Danny said with a sigh. "Just a tired singer short on luck."

The girl grinned at her. "Sing. Her." Her teeth appeared as if she'd been fed a steady diet of rocks. That may've accounted for the chittering sound the girl sometimes made. Danny hoped, once rescued, the girl would be whisked off to an oral surgeon, in addition to other medical specialists.

"C'mon," Danny said, "we have to keep going. Do I still need to drag you, or do you promise to follow?"

The girl nodded with a grin.

Danny released her arm and gestured. "Let's go. If I shout 'run,' you run. Okay?"

The girl nodded again.

With her staccato manner of speaking and odd reactions, Danny wasn't sure how much the girl really understood. She also wasn't sure how effectively the girl could run with those pencil-thin legs and wobbling knees.

They proceeded with more caution this time, Danny's thoughts darting as quickly as her eyes. She again saw the vending machines. Next to them, she saw a faded orange door, unmarked. She hadn't noticed it before, no doubt due to its dingy color; it was almost of a piece with the walls. In normal circum-stances, she would leave well enough alone. At the moment, she was willing to check any door not marked "Sudden Death." She gestured, and the girl followed close.

It was unlocked; a dim light shone from somewhere behind it. Danny slowly pushed the door open, wary that someone might be on the other side. She heard nothing, so she pushed it all the way, venturing a step forward. The door opened up onto a balcony. She stepped all the way in, moved all the way forward to peer over the railing.

Below were rows and piles of luggage. Suitcases, duffle bags, guitar bags, suitbags—almost every sort of traveling bag she could imagine. Some, closer to the room's edges, were lined up or stacked neatly on top of one another. Closer to the center were large mounds of bags, carelessly tossed.

There were hundreds. Several hundred. Danny wondered to whom they could possibly belong. Surely it couldn't have all been lost luggage? She scanned the area more closely, as well as the dim light and distance would permit. She thought she spotted her own red bag near a door, among the bags neatly lined up. If only she knew where the other side of that door was and could get down there and check . . .

She heard the girl chittering behind her. Danny regarded her and remembered. *Priorities.* They had to get outside first.

She closed the door and gestured for the girl to follow her as before. They continued on slowly, and slowed even more when the kiosks came into sight. The old creep had to be hiding behind one of them, maybe hiding *in* one of them, waiting to spring once she and the girl passed. Surely, he had the key to the cages. He probably had a key to everything that could be locked around here.

Danny moved closer to the wall and reached out, placing a hand on the girl's shoulder as they inched by, her sight glued to the kiosks, the pretzel one in particular. She remembered how she'd seen no sign of the hiding girl until she almost jumped on the poor thing. She wouldn't take her eyes off the kiosks, not until she reached the escalators.

The girl chittered. Danny looked and saw the girl was staring at something behind her. She turned. They were right next to the escalator. The old man was standing on the top step, two paces away, staring right back.

Danny shrieked, and the man wavered. Without thinking, she unslung her bag and heaved it toward his head while shouting, "Run!"

Not waiting to see if the old man was hit, or even whether the girl had started running on her own, Danny grabbed her by the wrist and hustled down the other escalator, ignoring the protesting sounds from the girl she was trying to protect. As they approached the automatic door, she was ready to push through but, to her surprise, she found it working. They didn't slow pace until they reached the glass-door exit in the baggage claim area. Danny hesitated but kept moving, barging into them. They were still unlocked. *Thank God.*

"Stop," the girl said. "*Stop!*"

Danny halted, panting. She looked at the girl, glanced toward the glass doors behind them, and then at the girl again.

"Hurt." The girl said the word, but made no gesture to indicate just where she was hurting. She only stood looking back toward the glass doors.

Danny tried to catch her breath. "S-sorry." As frazzled as she felt, she imagined the girl felt worse. She wanted to say that she was just trying to save her from further abuse, but for all she knew just saying the word or anything close would cause the girl to vividly remember the episodes. The girl was already upset; no need to upset her further. And no need for them to remain strangers.

"What's your name?" Danny asked.

The girl turned to her. She nodded as she spoke. "Knell. Uh."

Danny smiled. "That's cute. Don't worry, Nella." She pulled her phone out of her pocket and turned it on. "We'll be in happy land soon enough."

Reception—*finally.*

Danny kept her eyes on the glass doors as she dialed.

"*Nine-one-one. What's your emergency?*"

"Kidnapping! Child abu—" She took a breath. "Please just get the police out here now!"

"Okay, ma'am, calm down. Where are you calling from?"

"The airport. I'm at the airport."

"Which one?"

"I—" Danny didn't know. She patted her pockets. It had to be on her boarding pass, or on the map she'd picked up from the car rental desk . . . the map she'd stuffed into her bag, along with the boarding pass she'd stuffed in there when she'd originally boarded. *Shit.*

She looked around frantically for a sign, but saw nothing. She'd have to go back inside to grab another map.

"Ma'am? Ma'am, where are you? Which airport?"

"I'll tell you in a second. Hold on." Danny pantomimed for Nella to stay put as she started toward the doors. She'd run in, grab another map, and run right back out.

She got three steps before she saw him standing there, staring her down. Hanging over his left arm and shoulder was what appeared to be a rolled hose.

"Ma'am? What—?"

Her phone cut off. Dead.

She dropped it and spun around, reaching for Nella. She grabbed the girl's arm and started forward, in the general direction of the white van. When the van's bright headlights flicked on, she froze. Stark fear . . . paralyzed . . .

Danny could only remember how Nella first told her—*asked her*—to help her survive "them."

"Them" undoubtedly had her and Nella outnumbered, overpowered. Only wits would save the two of them. That, or a miracle.

It was a fool's hope but, pulling Nella with her, Danny headed into the field. A van didn't have to stay on the road, but she hoped there were some rocks or large branches or something otherwise that would make the terrain uneven and thus difficult for the vehicle. The maintenance man was slow. And even though he was a man, Danny figured she could hold her own in a confrontation, long enough at least for Nella to scramble away if she had sense enough to.

They'd gone a good distance, maybe even half a mile, before Danny's desire for uneven terrain backfired. She was nimble enough to let go of Nella before falling on her face, but she wasn't so quick to recover. She figured there'd be branches and rocks and potholes, but Danny had tripped over something as large as a log. She sat up, catching her breath while getting her bearings.

The van's lights were still on. She could see them in the far distance. It hadn't moved from the parking lot. There was no sign of the old man, either. She heard nothing other than her own breathing, her own heart rate—and Nella, chittering.

The girl needed help, more help than she was capable of giving. Danny still couldn't help but ask, "Are you alright?"

The only response was something hard and metallic slamming against the back of Danny's head.

DANNY KNEW the sun had risen before she even opened her eyes. She felt the early morning chill, the dew on her skin—all *over* her skin. She regretted the new day, more so when her eyelids parted.

She was still in the same field. She instinctively knew she was lying next to the object she'd tripped over before blacking out. She was facing its face—the face of one of the passengers who'd been on the plane with her. The record producer.

His eyes bugged out. His mouth hung open for a scream that would never come. His tongue protruded, touching the grass.

Danny supported herself on a shoulder and elbow, shooting daggers throughout her nervous system as she pushed up and got a better view of the man. Like her, he'd been stripped naked.

Unlike her, he'd been eviscerated. His entrails were inches away from her fingers.

She scrambled, backing away while trying to stand without touching any part of the butchery. She was on her buttocks but couldn't get to her feet before backing into something else. Her fingers felt something glutinous before she saw it. Although groggy, her mind was quick enough to grasp what it might be. Another passenger from her flight: denuded and disemboweled.

She shrieked as she forced herself to a standing position. Then, she didn't dare move.

Everyone who'd flown to this hellhole with her now surrounded her. All were massacred, mutilated. All of them except her. She alone . . . She—alone with the two other living figures standing just beyond the mass of bodies. The old man and Nella. Side by side.

The girl was naked but didn't seem at all bothered by the morning chill. A noose had been tied around her neck, undoubtedly by the old man. He held the other end, wrapped around his left arm and shoulder. The "hose" Danny had seen was more accurately some kind of cord. The man grasped a blue metallic rod in his other hand. It looked almost like an aluminum baseball bat, but it was about five feet long. Most likely it was the item that had knocked her cold. He raised it slightly as he stepped forward. Nella remained where she stood.

The old man avoided bodies and entrails without looking down even once. His eyes were focused on Danny's. She wanted to look away—she wanted *run* away—but she'd no will to move. She stayed put until the man stopped a few paces in front of her.

"Time for breakfast." The man spoke with a voice that made him sound twice as old as he looked. "Sing."

Danny was aghast.

"Sing." The man leveled the metal rod, pointing it just under her ribs, and jabbed. Danny felt the pain spiral several inches from the point of impact. She wanted to vomit.

"Sing."

The man kept jabbing her—in the ribs, under the ribs, in the sternum—while commanding her, gazing into her eyes without a single blink.

Danny didn't vomit. The prodding rapidly became less painful. Her midsection had gone numb.

She hadn't been exactly clear-headed when she awoke, and she was getting foggier with each passing moment. The man's eyes seemed to glow a luminescent yellow before flashing red, like emergency lights. Whether real or hallucinated, the flashes and the prodding pumped her insides. Her vessels and cords thrummed while something that had been dammed back prepared for its release.

She no longer had a choice. A poisonous frisson overtook her, as if her insides were being hurried over by millions of fiery insects. She opened her mouth wide, then let loose.

It started as possibly the most ungodly scream ever heard. The old man stumbled backward several feet at its force, falling backward over a corpse but without loosening his grip on either the rod or the cord. Danny's high-pitched scream lasted only a few seconds before descending into a powerful melody. It was then that Nella began to move. The girl didn't fall backward: She shook as if in the throes of an epileptic fit.

Danny wanted to run to her, but she couldn't move. She could only sing, and she couldn't stop.

She sang one long uninterrupted song through a range of styles, including the warbling style that had won her a loyal but small following in the Houston area—the same style that had won over the mysterious man on the other side of the phone just a few days prior.

She thought little now about whom that man could've been— it certainly wasn't the old man. Nella occupied her thoughts now. Nella, whose skin ripped open as the girl seized up and thrashed about. Nella, whose bones snapped and broke, to jut through the skin and reshape her arms and legs. Nella, whose jaw and face deformed itself. Nella, whose multiplying streams of blood sparkled like rivulets of crimson glitter.

Danny couldn't shut her eyes, couldn't shut out the sight of Nella spasmodically dancing to her song—leaping, tumbling to the ground, hopping, scratching, leaping into the air again—as her body changed, transmogrified into something with claws . . . with a beak . . . with arms twisted and pulled back behind her like a V.

The noose about her neck served its purpose. The old man had returned to his feet, caring nothing about Danny as he minded Nella and the cord. It was like a leash, made of material the girl couldn't break even as she grew wilder, clearly stronger, and less recognizably human. The rising sun appeared to lend support to the grotesque spectacle. In Danny's eyes, the sun's rays filtered into visible but free-floating strings in the girl's presence, jittering strings of nameless colors. Intentionally or not, the strings caught on the blood and stuck. They became more complex and took on patterns, as more accumulated.

Danny tried to push her song into another horrific scream. Instead, her voice simply switched into another melody as she witnessed what was once a frail, bruised girl complete her transformation into a large bird of broken flesh, fresh blood, light and shadow.

The creature was as tall as Nella had been, between five and six feet, but that was the only similarity. It still seemed to be in the middle of a fit as it flexed and fluttered its bright wings, feathers of light draping down her twisted, bony, bent-back arms. It perhaps would've flown away if not for the strong cord and impressive strength of the old man. He held the unruly cord with one hand as he grasped his rod in the other.

The creature flew up several feet and then fluttered down, landing near one of the mutilated bodies. It pecked among the innards until it caught the intestines in its beak. It wrestled with the entrails as if they were a living worm before managing to swallow them whole. It then picked and chose from among the other spillage before pecking at its own body and taking an abbreviated flight, alighting next to another corpse.

If only Danny could shut her eyes, shut her mouth, stitch them both shut . . . This was all some sort of devilish magic, something abominable that was somehow in some way being aided by her voice and possibly her very witness. But she couldn't shut up. She couldn't shut out the view.

The bird-like creature—Nella at its core—didn't seem quite finished with its transformation. It was beyond human, but the more Danny watched, the more it seemed to be trying to remake itself further. The sun even seemed complicit in the process.

The creature picked at the corpses and also pecked at its own body, rending itself, repairing itself—stitching with the thinnest rays of morning sunlight—dining and dancing, delighted by the song extorted through a torture Danny could never hope to describe with coherent words. And the bodies—the *nobodies*— that were ripped apart . . . What were the proper words for them? What more had they to lose?

Much more, it seemed.

Finished with the flesh, Nella hovered above the twice-over massacre and contributed a birdsong, pinching and altering it until reaching harmony with Danny, who in turn saw incorporeal forms rising from the corpses on the ground—appearing as irradiated insects of all shapes and sizes—floating upward toward Nella. Danny lost count after fifty. Nella then ceased her song and proceeded to snatch and swallow them all.

Breakfast. A feast on pieces of broken flesh and broken souls.

Danny stopped singing and fell to her knees. Though exhausted, she now understood. She understood her role in this black and sunny ritual—not as a singer, but as an instrument. The creature fed on both bodies *and* souls, and it needed the assistance of folks like Danny to live, to *survive*.

There'd be no assistance for Danny. She was through. Used up. She had no words, no pleas, no cries. Her throat was bone-dry.

Perhaps that's why the creature now appeared satiated. It alighted one last time and didn't even regard Danny. It turned its beak into its breast to rest while it molted light, slowly reverting to the form of a sleeping girl. An image from a fairy tale penned in Hell.

Danny's insides had been pushed to mush—nothing fit for a hellfowl. But maybe someone else was hungry . . .

The old man drove his rod into the ground with the strength of one three times his size. He wrapped his end of the cord around the pole, tethering the sleeping Nella to something sturdy lest she wake unexpectedly. He then turned his eyes back to Danny.

Almost totally expunged of anything resembling life, she let the man hoist her up like a sack of oats. He slung her over his shoulder and carried her away from the bodies, toward the green perimeter.

Only her eyes seemed to function. As she got closer, Danny saw it wasn't trees that encircled the meadow. It was a high barricade—a fence or a wall—overpopulated with green bags, each six to seven feet in length. Each one had been stuffed with something and strung up—for who-the-hell-cared what reason. Danny's nervous system could no longer tolerate answers.

The maintenance man carefully laid Danny's numb body on the grass. He stepped out of her range of vision for a few minutes and returned with a green bag draped around his shoulders. For a moment, he stood looking down at her with the same expression he'd worn when she first saw him. He was no janitor. He was a committed soldier of a long and secret war still ongoing.

The old man laid the bag beside Danny and unzipped it. He gently lifted her, and then placed her inside, face-up.

Danny wasn't the most sophisticated woman. There was so

much she didn't know or quite understand about this Brave Not-So-New World of 21st Century America. But she was smart enough to know that her ticket had not been to a town at all. Her real destination had been to some kind of facility. This whole set-up was some elaborate configuration designed to keep that body-and-soul-eater "Nella" alive. This went beyond the girl and the maintenance man. At the end of the day, they too were probably just like her—instruments in someone else's scheme, destined to be food for someone's twisted dream.

Before the zipper closed the bag over her eyes, Danny saw a passenger plane making its final descent. She wondered how many would be entertained for lunch.

HEAVEN'S GUN

The signs had been taped to each door on the first floor. Some rabble-ramble about there being a smoker on the floor . . . smoking being against condo rules, which had the effect of law . . . smoke endangering children . . . cops being called next time smoke was detected . . . *blah blah bluh.*

Jacob couldn't be bothered to read all five paragraphs. It was three-thirty in the morning. He'd already put in fourteen hours today. When he saw the screed taped to his own door, though, he was tempted to put in a few extra minutes bothering someone else.

He didn't consider himself exempt from condo community rules, but it seemed he was being singled out. Only the sign on his door had words underlined in red.

Cigarette smoke permeated the hallway as it always did in the late hours. Whoever the smoker really was—Jacob honestly didn't know or care—the fiend had probably stayed up to the wee hours and turned in an hour or two ago. Probably a double-shift worker like himself.

Jacob ripped the leaflet down from his door with one hand as he unlocked and turned the handle with the other. Sheila knew not to raise too much of a fuss at this hour. Like Jacob, she was a respectful tenant. But the bull terrier didn't hesitate to paw at his thighs while issuing whimpers almost as loud as barks.

"Sorry, girl." Jacob locked the door behind him. "You're on your own tonight." He knelt down to untie his Timberlands, trying to annoy rather than be annoyed by Sheila licking his hands and face. "Done all the walkin' I plan on doin' till I get some rest." He scratched her behind the ears as he stood. "C'mon."

He led Sheila to the patio door and opened it. The bull terrier looked out into the darkness, then back up at him. Jacob shook his head. Sheila again paused to look outside before reluctantly trotting out.

She'd roam, relieve herself, roam some more, then return when she was good and ready. She'd be gone for a minimum of ten minutes, a maximum of forty-five or so. She'd pick up the empty plastic bowl Jacob always left on the patio and tap it against the glass door—her secret knock—when she was ready to come in.

He was ready to relax. He turned on the stereo's CD player and pushed in a compilation of obscure blues singers singing slightly less obscure songs from the 1930s and 1940s. It was the only kind of music that could rub the knots out of his neck.

He leaned back in his recliner and closed his eyes, contemplating bourbon and sketching out the day ahead. He'd volunteered for the late-breakfast shift at the diner. It was a Friday, and late morning was the sweet spot—the time when a lot of the best paying customers began setting their plans for the evening. He had time for two, maybe two and a half hours of shut-eye before he needed to shower.

Someone banged on the front door, jolting him out of a reverie. He was expecting Sheila's tapping, or even barking. That he was used to. The pounding he'd heard instead gave birth to a minor headache.

He turned the music down on his way to the door, expecting a neighbor with a noise complaint. He looked out the peephole. One of two cops was staring back at him.

They weren't there to arrest him. He knew that protocol. The banging would've been fiercer and accompanied by the louder announcement and command: *Police! Open up!*

They could've been scammers. He knew that protocol as well. Crooks dressed up like cops, and when some unsuspecting chump opened the door, they'd beat and rob him.

He eyed his Glock on the bookshelf next to the door. He had strategically camouflaged and hidden it from casual observers behind a stack of books. Other guns were hidden around the apartment, including behind the stereo, but this was the closest. It was the easiest to reach if there were ever trouble on his doorstep.

It had been years since the possession of guns was made illegal for those outside law enforcement, but—at home or away—he always tried to keep one near his person. No need to have one in hand just yet, though. He was tired, but he was swift.

He cracked open the door. "Yes, officers?"

"We had a complaint."

"I turned the music down," Jacob said. "I'll keep it down."

"Not about that. About smoking."

"What?" Jacob's gaze shifted from one cop to the other. "I don't smoke."

"We had a complaint," the first cop said. "We have to follow up."

"Someone called building management," the second cop said, "and management called us. We agree some of these condo policies are a little silly, but in this state their rules have to be enforced by us."

"I *don't* smoke," Jacob said. "I can't afford to. I've already had one scare with my heart."

"Can we come in?"

Jacob didn't even glance at his bookshelf. He had enough close-up experience with cops—watching their movements, reading their badges, listening to their tone of voice—to know they were the real deal. If they'd seen him glancing, they would've become suspicious. No need to provoke them. Of course, they could've been corrupt cops, out to beat and rob him regardless. Most likely, he figured they were cops on the tail end of their late shift who had nothing better to do.

"Sure." Jacob stepped backward and opened the door wider. "Come on in." Normally he would've asked for a search warrant. But, again, no need to provoke.

The two men entered but didn't progress much beyond the doorway. Jacob kept his eyes on them as he made his way to the stereo. He turned it off but remained next to it, ready to grab the Glock behind it if necessary.

"Not much of a smell in here," the first cop said.

Jacob shook his head. "Only what you brought in with you."

The cops glared at him.

"And, me too," Jacob said. "The smoke is still on my clothes from when I got in a few minutes ago."

"Getting in from where?" the first cop asked.

"Work."

"Where do you work?"

"This an interrogation?" He'd humored them—they knew he wasn't the villainous smoker—but now he was tired of them. If they were going to make some kind of move, he wanted them to get on with it.

"Just asking," the second cop said. "You look familiar."

Jacob smirked. "I work at the diner on Baker Street. Maybe you've eaten there."

The cop stared and then nodded, but said nothing.

"And I've got to be back at work in a few hours," Jacob said, "so if you don't mind."

The cops exchanged glances. The second cop turned and put

his hand on the doorknob, then hesitated. It looked as if he were preparing to lock it.

Jacob took a step forward. On top of the stereo, his right hand inched toward the back edge, ready to snatch his piece. He could have it in hand, safety off, and pointed in less than two seconds.

The first cop wasn't looking at Jacob's hand. He seemed to be studying his face. Finally, he nodded and said, "Have a good night. Maybe we'll see you down at the diner soon."

They left without another word. Or glance.

Jacob locked the door behind them and looked out the peephole.

They were gone, or at least out of sight.

It didn't take long to figure who'd called them here in the first place: the Ethiopian, five doors down. Whoever the smoker was, Jacob was sure it was someone within two doors of that guy.

The Ethiopian . . . the same guy who'd refused to ever even nod "hello." The same guy who couldn't be bothered to hold the front door when Jacob's arms were burdened with groceries. The same guy with those three brats who ran up and down the halls when he was trying to nap. *He* was the one.

It took Jacob only a second or two longer to figure why the police had eyed him so. Did they know what he really did, or did they just catch his slip? The diner closed in the early evening and there was no way he could've just been getting home from work. Not unless he had another job.

He walked to the patio door and checked his watch. It was nearing four-thirty. Sheila should've been back already. Peering out, he saw nothing on the patio. Her tapping dish was untouched.

He'd entertained fears in the past. Letting Sheila run free, contrary to the city's leash laws, was just inviting someone to pick her up or poison her. But, even though she was his little sweetheart, Jacob knew no one could grab her without a fight, and she was too picky of an eater to be easily poisoned. No, she was a wily one. She'd taught Jacob a few tricks. The way his pre-dawn morning was turning out, however, he found it a little harder to push away dread.

He grabbed a jacket and flashlight, left two lamps on, then locked the patio door behind him. He knew Sheila's favorite and less traveled routes. He followed one of them at random while calling her name.

He entered the woods, treading a dirt path frequented by dog-walkers and joggers. It stretched on for miles, winding behind several housing complexes. He wasn't worried about waking anyone. The early risers were already waking, turning on their lights and radios and getting ready for work. Buses were beginning their routes, and garbage trucks would soon join them. One man calling a woman's name wouldn't bother anyone.

But Sheila didn't respond. Despite the flashlight, Jacob stumbled more than once, mixing curses with her name, which didn't help. It was ten minutes before he saw his little girl, pacing in front of a dense cluster of ferns and stopping every so often to issue a whimpering bark.

"Sheila? What is it?"

The bull terrier barked again but didn't even glance in his direction.

Jacob approached, looking around him. Beyond several rows of trees was a middle school. On the other side were three-story houses. Upper middle class territory.

Standing next to her, he asked again, "What is it, Sheila?"

She hunched down, pointing her nose. Jacob crouched. He used the flashlight and his free hand to untangle the weave of vegetation until he saw it. He blinked a few times and shook his head, something in him not wanting to believe he was staring at a gun.

It was black, the color of starless midnight, hard to really distinguish even with the flashlight shining on it. At first glance, it resembled a Colt Anaconda, but he knew it wasn't. It wasn't quite like any other revolver or even any other handgun he'd ever seen. Even on the current black market, where all kinds of firearms from the past hundred years could be found relatively easily, this thing would've been an oddity. He couldn't resist picking it up.

It was ice cold, but Jacob grasped instead of dropping it. He was surprised the handle warmed almost instantly and to such a degree that the warmth enveloped his hand. It was as if he'd put on a glove. He ran his left hand over the barrel. It didn't feel like metal; it was more like some kind of tough plastic, radiating warmth.

He heard two separate rustles in the treetops—one in the tree directly above him and one nearby. There was no breeze, and the commotion sounded like much more than what a squirrel could manage. Tiredness and confusion may have been feeding his paranoia, but he thought it best to move away quickly.

He tucked the gun into his jacket's holster. Worried over Sheila, he'd made the rare mistake of leaving his pad while unarmed. If there were someone in the woods who meant him harm, he wanted something in his possession.

He rationalized his taking the gun in retrospect when he was halfway home and realized he still had it. The initial grab had been done out of pure instinct, part of a basic will to survive. Sheila had kept up as he ran and, at the halfway point, took the lead.

He hustled after her. He hadn't heard any other noises behind him, but the right side of his chest, which was closest to the gun, felt warm. There was something special about the piece. He wanted to get home, safely, and examine it.

He checked behind him before he stepped onto his patio. Nothing.

He let Sheila inside, looked around again, then locked the patio door behind him. He pulled the blinds over the glass then headed toward the kitchen.

He laid the gun on the counter. He expected it to be glowing, but it remained black as obsidian. He stared at it for a moment, trying to figure the source of the warmth—as if sight alone would tell him—before he decided to open the cylinder. It'd be a good idea to check if the piece were loaded, and with what.

The gun was again ice cold but warmed instantly like before. An oddity, but it was nothing compared to what he saw when examining the cylinder. Each chamber appeared as if it were the inside of a tiny geode.

What the hell had he picked up?

His head jerked at the sound of a piercing screech coming from his bedroom.

The alarm clock. The alarm near his recliner would sound off in ten minutes. Jacob checked his watch. No hope of getting any decent shut-eye at this point. He decided he may as well head out to the diner early.

He carried the gun with him as he shut off the alarms. He then took it with him into the bathroom. Strange as the thing was, he wanted it near him. He allowed a significant distance only when he left it on the sink during the five minutes he spent in the shower. Even then, he did his best to keep an eye on it through the transparent shower curtain.

He dressed quickly then put out some food for Sheila. All the while, the bull terrier kept her eyes trained on the gun in her master's waistband. "Be back around four for dinner," he told her.

Thankfully, it was a crisp day. He could wear his work jacket over his regular outfit and no one would question it. Like many of his other jackets, it had a hidden holster that would cradle his new baby quite nicely. He usually didn't carry at work, just kept a piece in his car. But he wasn't going to part with his new foundling. Not until he knew more about it.

He set his apartment's alarm and walked out the front door. Down the hall, the Ethiopian was hustling his kids out of the apartment, no doubt preparing to escort them to the bus stop.

On any other morning, Jacob would've turned away and

headed for the floor's other exit. Today, something impelled him to approach.

The Ethiopian seemed to notice him only after all the kids had been shuffled into the hall. After closing and locking his door, he turned to find Jacob almost nose-to-nose with him. Neither man moved.

"Call the cops on me again," Jacob said, "and I'll give you a damn good reason to."

Jacob turned and walked toward the farther exit. He restrained himself from shoving any of the kids out of his way. He tried to walk as straight a line as possible, hoping the Ethiopian would call his bluff. Instead, he heard the man nervously whispering to his kids, hurrying them toward the closest exit.

The left side of Jacob's chest felt warm. He smiled.

JACOB SCANNED THE CUSTOMERS, again, as he wiped the counter. From his first day on the job, he'd spent every free moment studying people—their faces, their clothes, their body language, their dietary preferences . . . everything he could think of. It helped him better serve his customers. He knew the regulars. He knew what they wanted to eat as soon as they stepped in the door based on the time of day and what they were wearing. At this point, he even had a good feel for strangers. He could guess what they might want just by the way they walked and their expressions. He was right fifty percent of the time.

Studying people and pegging them correctly served him well as an assistant manager in the restaurant business. The talent served him even better in a more lucrative side business.

Today, among sixteen regulars, he spotted four plainclothes cops—one or two were possibly undercover, two were clearly detectives—and three cops sporting the shameful uniforms of beat walkers.

He knew one of the plainclothes and two of the men in uniform; he'd often chatted with them. In the guise of small talk —and while offering copious amounts of free coffee for the services they provide to the community—he learned as much as he could about their daily routine and that of their fellow officers without appearing suspicious.

Brennan, the diner's owner, had had several brilliant ideas. One was to create an establishment that served as a fast food joint for those on the go and an old-school diner experience for those eating in. Cops were generally drawn to the latter experience, whereas customers on the opposite side of the fence were drawn to the former. Another brilliant idea was to establish the joint just two blocks away from the police station. The place always had four or more cops as sit-down customers, and they were treated exceedingly well: free coffee and pastries and half off everything else. The badges were comfortable in here. Here, they let down their guard.

Jacob made eye contact with a man as he pushed through the left side entrance. Five o'clock shadow. Late thirties. Dark-wash jeans, sports jacket over a button-down . . . hip guy with a hip job taking an early lunch . . . because he could afford to take lunch whenever he wanted without being reprimanded. He made decent money. He was willing to spend money on indecencies. He was a Johnny-Mark. The two darting rightward movements of his eyes when Jacob made contact were as good as a secret handshake.

Jacob casually made his way to his register and signaled to all those waiting that it was open for business. The diner usually kept only one register open. The second was opened either when cops entered and signaled they were in a hurry or when the line at the first register was more than nine people long. The line had been twelve-people deep before Jacob stepped up.

The Johnny-Mark got in Jacob's line. When it became the Johnny-Mark's turn to order, Jacob clutched the side of the register with his left hand and curled the ring finger just so while letting the pinky stick straight out.

"Would you like to try the number six?" Jacob asked.

"I would like to try the number nine, *special*," the Johnny-Mark said.

"Chicken, beef, pork, or—"

"Beef."

"How would you like your eggs?"

"Over easy."

"Drink?"

"Coffee. With cream and sugar."

"Carry out, or—?"

"Dine in."

"Got it, chief," Jacob said with a nod. "Your number's on your receipt. Please step to the left."

The exchange could've gone any number of ways. There were many combinations Jacob and the customer could've used.

As the Johnny-Mark had given him the key terms, Jacob had pushed the appropriate buttons on the register. The folks in the back would prepare the customer's food, exactly as ordered, but on his tray, under a protective sheet, they'd include another sheet detailing the profiles of the type of girl he'd ordered for later that evening.

Special nine over six? The customer wanted *real* action. Beef over chicken or pork? He wanted his action figure to have curves where it counted, not model thin or big and beautiful. Eggs over easy? He wanted the girl to pamper him like a king, or a father. He didn't want scrambled—give-and-take rough sex—or fried—a girl who would essentially play dead while he did anything and everything short of actually killing her. Coffee with cream and sugar? He wanted an ethnic girl—but not too ethnic, preferably a mixed girl or someone who was at least light skinned. Dine in? In-call at a decent hotel rather than in-call at a cheap motel.

It was never too difficult to fit the specifications of a Johnny-

Mark's desires—not as difficult as it should've been, considering Jacob's partners offered girls only under the age of eighteen. Jacob knew there were five or six girls who fit the profile of what this Johnny-Mark had specified. All of them would be on the sheet. After finishing his meal and leaving, the Johnny-Mark would review the profiles, make his choice, and then call the number on the sheet. Calls only. No text messages. The man who answered—one of Brennan's brothers—wanted to hear the voice of whomever he was speaking to. Certain telltale signs would result in him clicking off the phone, disposing of it, and calling the whole thing off. But the Johnny-Marks who weren't cut off gave the brother a series of three numbers—the same numbers on the receipt—that, when deciphered, gave three pieces of information: the proposed time of the appointment, the amount of time proposed for the appointment, and the base amount the Johnny-Marks were willing to spend, which was never under fifteen hundred. In turn, they received a series of numbers that, when deciphered, gave the time of the appointment, name of the location, and the number and time to call to get more details. Specifics would be nailed down during the second call.

It was a complicated code, but it had to be. Thanks to the law known euphemistically as the Mistress Act, anyone involved in a pay-to-play sexual activity was guaranteed a minimum three-year prison sentence. One strike and you were in. The multiple levels of screening served to protect the operation and its customers, and the customers were invariably the types who had or were willing acquire whatever funds necessary to enter the playground.

Jacob had already served time in jail for armed robbery and assault. He had no interest in serving time in the type of places they housed sex offenders. In holes like that, getting raped by a gang of fellow prisoners was the least of one's worries.

But he wasn't worried about anything today. The Johnny-Mark he'd just served had given off no weird vibes, nor had the two others who'd come in before him. Jacob watched as the guy nonchalantly ate his meal. The cops in the diner paid him no mind.

It'd been a very good day so far. His heart felt warm.

JACOB and his partners used only hotels or motels. Never residences, not even those located in less populated areas. It was far too risky.

Hotels and motels carried their own risks, but they were manageable. There were only ten that his partners would use. All the managers and relevant staff were paid off with drugs, girls, or money, usually a combination. And his partners thoroughly checked the premises at least one hour prior to an appointment. When Jacob was overseeing, he used his talents to size up everyone he saw, doing his best to detect any pigs in sheep's clothing.

Presently, he was overseeing his third appointment of the evening, the first one at a hotel.

His boys were already in position. One man was watching the parking lot. Another was pretending to read in the lobby. Men were in the stairwells, and one was posted in the elevator bank on the ground floor. All of them had guns and tablets. All of them were poised to ping him if they saw anyone suspicious. There was also a man in the room adjacent to the girl's. Jacob would join him soon.

He knocked the secret knock on the girl's door.

Desiree opened the door as far as the chain would allow and peeked through the crack.

"Let me in," Jacob said.

The girl vacantly gazed at him for more than a moment before closing the door. She unhooked the chain and slowly reopened the door, allowing Jacob just enough room to slide through.

She was wearing pink panties and a white lace camisole, one Jacob had little trouble seeing through in spite of the room's dim lighting.

"How do you feel?" he asked.

Her eyelids fought to stay apart as she nodded. Jacob could tell she'd just taken the Jelly Raptures. She should've swallowed them twenty minutes ago. Unlike many of the other fifteen-year-olds his partners managed, this one needed a little extra schooling.

All girls were instructed to take a combination of Raptures about thirty minutes prior to meeting a Johnny-Mark. It took roughly twenty-five minutes for the effects to kick in. The right combination of the colored beans—in this case, two yellows with red speckles, two red-and-blue striped, and one golden brown with a single ivory dot—would help make the girl more compliant, more sensual, while remaining cognizant enough to read the cues of the Johnny-Mark, knowing when to go slow and when to push for the release.

Desiree may have waited too long to pop the beans. Jacob couldn't afford for her to be sloppy tonight.

"Anything I need to know about?" he asked.

The girl shook her head like a content cat. He took that as her answer.

"You feelin' as you should?" he asked. "You know what you need to do?"

The girl stepped forward and put her hand on his elbow. "Jake . . . Big Jake . . . I need . . ."

"What?" he said. "More?" It was easy enough to get anyone hooked on the Raptures. After all, they looked and tasted like fancy jellybeans. Pretty, sweet, and thoroughly corrupting. Just as any good drug should be—or any good trick, for that matter. But allowing a trick to go beyond her limit, especially one who was still a child in body and mind, was just asking for trouble that couldn't be easily handled.

Still, promises had to be made all around for the man in charge of this appointment to get what he wanted. "You'll get more JRs after you give the JM his happy ending."

The girl shook her head. "No . . . need to . . . *want* . . . to go home . . ."

Jacob chuckled. "Honey, you get to travel forever. That's what everyone stuck at 'home' wants. That's why you left yours, remember? You set out for adventure. Now you're in Heaven. All the pure pleasure you can get. Don't forget that."

". . . so tired . . ."

He shook his head. "Not tonight, you're not."

The girl swayed as if she were about to fall on her face. Jacob put her hands in his.

"Desiree, listen. I won't let anything happen to you. You do your job and I'll do mine. You can sleep in a few hours."

His phone chirped. He pulled it out of his pocket and looked at the text. One of his partners had messaged that the Johnny-Mark was on his way up the elevator. Jacob checked the time on his phone. It was ten till ten. No hope of stalling him, not without arousing suspicion and scaring him away. He could only hope the drugs punched in sooner than usual.

He squeezed Desiree's hands. "Perform well—get this jackass to cough up three grand—and I'll give you tomorrow off. The entire day. Okay?"

The girl's head dropped. A half-hearted nod. That'd have to do for his answer. Best thing for him to do now was just get the hell out of the way and let her do her job. She'd done it often enough. She knew how to play. Jacob led her toward the bed and positioned her like a lounging Lolita.

As he left the room, he heard the elevator opening down the hall. He retrieved his key card and ducked into the adjacent room just as he saw the Johnny-Mark rounding the corner.

The man in the room nodded. "Heard this guy's a first-timer."

Jacob walked to stand behind him and gazed at the laptop monitor. "Everyone has a first time. Desiree's good. She'll have him beggin' to come back."

Both men watched the monitor. Two strategically placed cameras and three equally camouflaged microphones in Desiree's room ensured them a relatively complete picture of anything that happened in the room. The laptop could adjust the picture to compensate for the dim lighting. If the Johnny-Mark got out of hand, they'd see or hear and be on him in less than a minute. Jacob had brought two guns. The mystery one remained close to his heart, in his jacket's holster. His loaded Glock was tucked in his waistband at the small of his back. He hoped to keep it there. He and his partners wanted a long, uninterrupted performance that they could post online later.

The Johnny-Mark knocked the customer's knock on Desiree's door. She rose languidly from the bed and seemed to slide into character as she moved easily toward the door. It was too dark to read her facial expression, but the tone of voice seemed right as she said, "Coming."

After cracking the door to peep through, she let the man in. Dim light notwithstanding, there was no mistaking his smile. He was dressed all in black, with a jacket Jacob thought a little too heavy for the weather. Oh, well—the Johnny-Marks all had their little quirks. Jacob was more concerned with what he was carrying that with what he was wearing.

Along with the all-important greeting card, Johnny-Marks often brought flowers or candy to their hosts. The kinkier ones brought toys. This one could've brought any of the above; the greeting card was taped to a container the size of a shoebox. First-timers were usually so nervous they tended to overcompensate.

"Switch to split-screen mode," Jacob said. "We don't want to miss anything."

"What the hell'd he bring her?" his partner asked as he switched the view. "A chocolate bunny?"

Desiree put one hand on the man's shoulder and another on the strap of her camisole as she kissed him on the cheek. He turned away to place the box on top of the dresser.

"Is that for me?" Desiree sultrily asked.

The Johnny-Mark turned toward her. "Mind if I get more comfortable?"

"Of course not, baby," Desiree purred. "Need some help?" She stepped forward and laid her hands on his jacket collar. He stepped back while removing her hands.

"I need to use the bathroom first . . . Maybe you want to join me? I may need an extra hand."

"Great," Jacob's partner said. "Another water-sports freak. He indicate that this morning?"

"No," Jacob said. "And he ain't gettin' it tonight."

Desiree giggled then raised her index finger in front of her face; she wagged it as she sexily shook her head. *Good girl*, Jacob thought. No matter what was asked, a girl always had to decline in a way that wouldn't upset the Johnny-Mark. The goal, after all, was always to squeeze as much money out of them as possible. Angry men didn't like to spend a lot of money. Jacob was happy the Raptures hadn't affected Desiree's memory. She knew what the man had ordered and what he hadn't. Jacob and the other handlers always took special care to coach his girls prior to their appointments.

The man closed the bathroom door behind him—all the way. Jacob furrowed his brow. This guy was giving off some funny vibes, far different from what he picked up as he took the guy's order that morning. The Johnny-Mark didn't appear nervous; it was something else. He hadn't kissed or even hugged the girl. Nor did he remove his jacket after he entered the room. What kind of Johnny-Mark wore his jacket into the bathroom?

Desiree glanced at the bathroom door then hurried over to

the dresser. She pulled the envelope off the box, opened it, and peered inside. A pained expression spread across her face.

"What—?" Jacob's partner began.

Jacob tensed.

Desiree plucked out the greeting card, opened it, cursed, and tossed it to the floor. She then peered inside the envelope again, cursed again, and ripped it in half. Both the card and the envelope had been empty.

Jacob saw the look on her face and wished he could shout through the wall—*Stay cool, girl. He may have all the money on him, or it may be in the box.*

Most Johnny-Marks laid the base amount—tucked in a greeting card—on the table when entering; they kept the tip—usually sizable—on their person. The break in protocol seemed to confuse her. Staying cool was the thing Desiree was least prepared to do.

The bathroom door opened. The man was still fully clothed, jacket and all. Desiree turned toward him and shouted, "Where the fuck is the money?" The purr had become a growl.

"What?"

She started toward him. "I asked about the money, asshole! Where the fuck is it?"

A fail on two counts. The girl had obviously taken the wrong combination of Raptures, and perhaps too many. She was far angrier than she should've been, far angrier than Jacob had ever seen her. Not to mention careless. She knew she was to never mention money during an appointment.

"Money for what?" the man asked.

"No, Desiree, don't—" Jacob muttered as he took another step backward. He realized what was happening a moment before she said it.

"Did you want me to fuck you or not?" Desiree hollered. "Cuz you ain't gettin' shit without my money!"

"What?" the man said. "You mean you want money for sex? With that body?"

The girl lunged at him. The man sidestepped, palmed her face, and shoved her toward the bed. Desiree got up as quickly as she went down and rushed at him again. The man's hand went into his jacket and pulled out a taser. Desiree probably wouldn't have stopped even if she were fully aware of what was happening. The man shot her in the stomach without a word. Desiree's screaming said enough for the both of them.

It had all happened so quickly. Jacob had started toward the door as soon as the man said "sex." But the action on the screen played out in less than twenty seconds.

"All gone to hell," he said as he rushed out into the hall. He paused before he reached Desiree's door.

Two menacing figures were at the far end of the hall to his left. He turned. Two more figures, similarly outfitted, were down the hall to his right. They were covered in black from head to toe —from *helmet* to *boot*—and carrying semiautomatic pistols.

There was no trace of skin, no exposed areas on any of them. Nevertheless, he reached his right hand behind him.

"*Freeze!*" They all pointed their weapons at him. "Heartland Security! *Don't* move!"

Jacob froze. His mind boiled. This whole damn thing was a setup. The man in Desiree's room was either a Heartland Security agent or some kind of informant working with them. And he was well trained; Jacob hadn't detected even a hint of pig or rat in the diner. His boys downstairs hadn't warned him because they were either already subdued or they had been in on it from the beginning. And, of course, the jack-booted thugs had the means to convince the hotel staff to participate . . . Heartland Security —*not* cops. The Heartland Security Agency took the Mistress Act more seriously than local authorities, but surely they had more important things to do than come down on Jacob and his crew.

He held his position as the agents on either end steadily

approached. In front of him, Desiree's door opened. The undercover stood in the doorway, holding the box he'd brought with him in both hands. Now in better light, Jacob saw it was neither a box of candy nor a box containing a toy. It wasn't even cardboard. It was metal plated. It was a container for something serious.

The man smirked at Jacob. "You know, we're not some bumfuck cops. We've known about your shitty little code for months. Deciphered the whole damn thing in less than a week. We know exactly what you and your pals have been doing."

Jacob was puzzled. He was careful not to make any sudden moves, but he noticed the agents on either end were still approaching very deliberately. The man in the doorway wasn't moving closer. It was almost as if they were afraid of Jacob.

Though they'd said nothing about it, he knew about his right to remain silent—but curiosity overwhelmed him. "Why didn't you ever take us down before?"

"You're small fish," the man said. "We only go after the big ones."

That meant they were after Brennan, the man at the top of the entire organization. He and his brothers had been involved with prostitution, drugs, and gun running long before they ever even set up shop in the area. Though Jacob had climbed a few steps in the organization, he'd never been part of the innermost circle. But—his thoughts still churning—he figured something had happened recently that had made him into something of a shark.

The agents on either side of him were no more than fifteen feet away. Not only his mind but his chest was burning. He couldn't remain still.

He rushed the man in the doorway. The man was taken off guard and, his hands full, easily taken to the ground. Jacob rolled off of him, slammed the door shut, and drew his Glock.

The man scrambled to get to his feet as he reached inside his jacket.

"Freeze," Jacob growled. "I see your hand come out, I pull the fuckin' trigger."

The man kept his hand where it was as he straightened. "They're going to come through that door any second, you know. They have a key card. You can't get out of this."

"What do you want?" Jacob asked.

"Lay your weapon down and we'll go easy on you. I promise."

Jacob glanced at Desiree. She wasn't moving. It appeared she wasn't even breathing. "You didn't go easy on her."

"What do you care?" The man seemed less frightened, more indignant now. "She's a child that you pimped out for sex. Just a sex slave you and your crew were holding prisoner."

"You didn't give a damn about her. Look at what *you* did. Treatin' her as a means to an end. You tell me what the end is."

The agent said nothing. Jacob wondered if his partner in the next room were sitting there listening, recording all this. Not that it mattered. The agents had seen Jacob come out of that room. They'd rush it and take down his partner soon enough. Fuck him, anyway.

"I'm no good guy," Jacob said, "but neither are you. I want to know exactly what you want from me, then I'll decide whether it's worth my time to cooperate."

There was a banging on the door. "You're out of time," the man said as he jerked his hand out of his jacket and aimed.

Jacob fired, plugging the man in the forehead.

The agents outside burst into the room.

Jacob turned and fired while scrambling for cover behind the bed, behind Desiree's body.

The agents' body armor withstood all bullets. Three of them took aim. Jacob ducked before they fired.

The bed was high enough off the ground for him to slide under. He could think of no other out.

He gained a few seconds, but now he was trapped. Done for. His Glock had one bullet left, and it wouldn't do him any good.

These guys were armored up tight. His armor was nothing but khakis, t-shirt, and a jacket.

His chest throbbed. His heart was burning . . . The *gun*. That's what they were after.

But he couldn't get to it. No way now to pull it out and see what was so special about the damned thing. No—he had just one play left.

"I give up!" He shouted it until he heard the only words he wanted to hear.

"Come out slowly! To your left! Keep your hands empty and keep them visible at all times!"

"Coming!" he shouted back. "I'm leaving the Glock here under the bed! Don't shoot! I'm coming peacefully!"

Jacob laid the Glock on the floor to his right and edged his body toward the left.

"Keep your hands where we can see them!"

His widespread left hand was the first thing he slid out from under the bed. One of the agents grabbed it and pulled, dragging the rest of him out.

Jacob lay flat on his back, exposed, staring up at the three firearms pointed at him. The fourth agent stood at his head. His gun was holstered.

"Backup is on the way," the fourth agent said. "We should just shoot you. You killed one of our agents. All of your people in this building are either dead or in custody."

Jacob almost said out loud, *Then why don't you just kill me?* It'd be a far better fate than an HSA-run prison.

"But we're still willing to give you a break. One last chance. Keep your hands where we can see them and stand up slowly."

He did as asked, though he didn't trust for one second they were going to give him a break.

The four surrounded him, one agent on either side, one in front, and one behind.

"You took something earlier today," said the agent to his right, the one who'd holstered his weapon. "Something that you found in the woods. I am asking you to hand it over."

"If you knew what I had, why didn't you pull me at the diner?"

The agent laughed. "Well, if we were going to move on you, we figured we might as well move on your little operation as well."

Yeah, if they took him down in the restaurant, Brennan and his brothers had several protocols in place to minimize damage to the rest of the organization. If the feds had known about Brennan for months, they had probably been waiting for the right time to move and shut down the whole thing. This wasn't that time, but they couldn't wait any longer. Or, at least, *these* feds couldn't. Jacob hadn't seen a single badge. He'd no doubt that they were HSA, but this was a dark unit. They'd moved tonight to take out a few pushers and pimps simply as cover, for public consumption. They were really here for just one purpose.

"If I hand it over?" Jacob asked.

"As I said, we'll give you a break."

Jacob had never dealt with HSA agents before, but he'd had enough experience with law enforcement to know how to read between the lines. The only break these assholes would give him would be between the shoulders and skull. They knew he had their gun—why didn't they just cuff him, frisk him, and *take* it?

He had an advantage. They knew it. And, now, so did he.

"It's inside my jacket," Jacob said. "It's not loaded. I'll take it out and throw it on the bed."

"No," the agent to his left said. "You'll take it out and place it in the box—*slowly*."

The agent to his right backed up and picked the rectangular box off the floor. He opened it and approached. Jacob looked inside.

It *was* a containment box—specifically for the gun. These hardened agents, even with their gloves and armor, were afraid to touch the weapon.

He wasn't.

He slowly brought his right hand down. "Takin' it out now. Just ease up, alright?"

Far as he could tell, each agent took exactly one step back—no more—as he reached inside his jacket. He wondered if any of these goons had been in the diner this morning. Had he served any of them breakfast? If so, he wondered what they'd eaten. If only he could see their faces . . . *Uptight assholes.* Constipated types like them should be eating oatmeal.

His fingers grasped the handle. It not only felt as if he'd slipped on a glove. It felt as if the glove were alive, and intelligent.

The agent behind him said, "Slowly . . ."

Jacob whipped the gun out and fired at the first helmet he saw and spun and fired at the next and the next. He only paused when aiming at the fourth agent, the one holding the box. For a moment, Jacob thought he could see through the black face shield; he thought he saw the expression of stark terror one second before he pulled the trigger. He stood watching as the face shield shattered, as if in slow motion, revealing a face spurting and gushing a lumpy gray liquid out of the nostrils, ears, and eyes.

Horrified and fascinated at once, Jacob remained rooted, gaping as the agent slumped and fell backward, the lumpy liquid continuing to spill as its pace eased from gush to ooze.

He weighed the gun in his hand. He didn't look at it. He was afraid to, briefly entertaining the notion that if he did, it might do something horrible to his face, to his *head*.

He turned his attention to the other agents. They'd met the same fate as their fallen partner—helmets shattered open, heads leaking gratuitous amounts of brain matter, matter that had been reduced to *oatmeal*.

The gun. The gun loaded with what-in-God's-name did this.

He heard distant voices coming from the hall. More agents were on the way. He had to move.

He cast an eye at the open containment box and considered carrying it with him. But what the hell for?

Have gun, will travel.

He ran out of the room. Pairs of agents were on either end of the hall. They must've been coming up the stairwells.

"Freeze!"

"Drop your weapon!"

"Don't move!"

Scramble 'em. Jacob didn't take much thought to aim. He just pointed, fired, spun, and repeated. Each targeted body, when hit, exploded in a mess of blood, bones, and armor.

He'd gotten them all before any of them could get off a shot. But he wasn't one to wait around and admire his work. He turned to his right and bolted for the stairwell.

He pushed through the door and paused, his weapon ready. The stairwell was free of agents, but he had to descend ten flights before hitting fresh air. He could be ambushed at any second.

To hell with 'em all. To hell with their numbers, their armor, and their authority. He had the advantage. He had a gun that was a gift directly from *Heaven*.

He hustled down the stairs, hopping down two or three at a time when he could. He was approaching the seventh floor when the door opened. Someone was entering the stairwell.

A man, in plain clothes. Jacob couldn't tell if he was just a man or an agent. And he certainly couldn't wait for the man to pull a weapon.

Jacob aimed his gun and pulled the trigger. The man's head exploded in a fine red and yellow mist. Jacob leapt over the headless fool and tried to quicken his pace.

He made it to the bottom of the stairwell without further interruption, but he halted before pushing through the exit door.

The parking lot would be crawling with agents. He wasn't wearing any kind of armor. He wasn't invulnerable. One fool just had to get off one lucky shot and it'd be all over for him. He had to play this smart.

The agents upstairs hadn't shot him because they either wouldn't or couldn't touch the gun. He hoped the same trick would work twice.

He pushed through the door. Bright spotlights switched on directly in front of him, blinding him. He raised his left arm over his eyes.

"Freeze!"

"Don't move!"

"Lower your arm!"

He slowly lowered his arm and was careful not to make any sudden moves. He was forced to squint in the face of the too-bright lights. He couldn't see how many agents there were. He couldn't see *where* they were.

"Slowly place your weapon on the ground—now!"

No. The gun belonged to him. It was a *part* of him. He felt it in his very heart, deep in his soul. But a thought struck. An idea. He hoped it was more than a whim. He prayed his new sense was leading him down the right path.

He slowly stooped and laid the gun on the ground.

"Lock your hands behind your head and kick the gun away from you!"

He did as instructed.

"Now get on your knees!"

He again followed orders.

"Don't move!"

He didn't. And, though still squinting, he finally saw agents entering his view. A few to the left, a few to the right, and some behind. None of them were his immediate concern. His main attention was on those approaching from the front. He didn't try to count how many. He was just waiting for enough of them to cross the paths of the spotlights, allowing him to see.

There.

He opened his eyes wide and focused on the gun, still lying on the ground. He concentrated. It shook. He sent it a thought. It began sliding in his direction.

Several agents noticed and shouted. Several more rushed forward.

Jacob *shoved* a thought at the gun. It hurtled itself toward him.

Jacob grabbed the gun, ducked, rolled, and came up to a knee, firing at every moving thing that crossed his field of vision. When it felt right, he rolled again, shifted position, and fired again.

The shouting shifted to screaming as agents exploded, collapsed in upon themselves, or experienced some other fatal torture. Blood flowed like milk or eased like syrup as some of the closer agents were riddled—puffed and flattened at once—like waffles.

Jacob hustled to his feet, running and shooting, as he made for the nearest cluster of parked cars. When he managed to hunker down between two vehicles, he heard two voices: the only two agents left alive. One screamed at the other to call for backup. The other shouted that they should just lay down heavy fire and put Jacob down.

He couldn't let them do either.

He'd gotten this far because no one wanted to touch the gun, and, once he began firing, the other agents were too shocked and awed at the results to effectively counterattack. These two remaining had gotten over their surprise. They'd kill him and figure out the rest later.

He'd have to regain the element of surprise.

He flattened himself on the ground and looked under the car toward the voices. One agent was approaching. Jacob wasn't sure where the other one was. Didn't matter. He had the general position of one. He just had to draw his attention.

He turned to his side and pointed the gun straight in the air. He pulled the trigger. Several hundred feet up, a flare exploded.

Jacob stood, aimed over the car's hood at the confounded agent, and pulled the trigger.

It was as if a cannonball traveling at light speed had hurtled through the agent's midsection. He looked like a human-shaped donut as he teetered before falling to the ground.

I'll reduce the other one to hash, Jacob thought. But the other agent wasn't in view. Jacob didn't hear anything, either.

To hell with it. The other one probably ran away with wet pants. Jacob certainly wasn't going to chase him down. He instead hustled toward his SUV. He needed to get home and do a little thinking before making his next move.

As he neared the vehicle, he slowed his pace and checked out his surroundings.

Nothing.

No one.

The HSA must have cleared the lot before he arrived and ordered everyone to stay inside the hotel till they gave the all clear. That signal was going to come long after Jacob had left.

He unlocked his vehicle and settled himself inside. He started it up and laid the gun on the front passenger's seat. He checked all windows and mirrors before shifting into drive.

That last agent really must have run away. Jacob was free and clear. Even when he hit the road and exceeded the speed limit by twenty, he didn't see any flashing lights in the rearview.

But they'd come. They weren't just going to let him walk away with this—this gun from Heaven. Their second wave would be superior to the first. He'd have to be ready. He'd have to try to truly *understand* the gun.

Hell, what was there to understand? He pointed the gun, pulled the trigger, and it transformed his thoughts—subconscious if not conscious—into results. His aim didn't even have to be spot on, just close enough.

He could really go places with this. But he had to deal with the present before plotting a future.

He parked the SUV in his complex's lot. He placed Heaven's piece in his jacket and got out of the vehicle. He pushed the button on his keychain to lock it, then he smelled something.

Smoke. It was coming from him.

He checked the inside of his jacket. It wasn't burning, not even warm. But the smoke was coming from the gun. It didn't smell like gun smoke. It smelled more like incense. Jacob couldn't pin down the exact scent, but it grew heavier, thicker, as he made his way to the side entrance of the building. He was almost suffocating in the aroma as he walked the hall toward his front door.

Sheila was waiting for him as always when he entered, but she kept her distance, issuing only one bark when Jacob stepped inside.

"You need a walk," Jacob said, "and so do I."

He headed straight for the patio door. Sheila bolted out when he opened it. He didn't run after her. After locking the door behind him, he followed her route, but at his own pace.

His heart was as warm as usual when the gun was close to his chest. Beyond that, he and his jacket weren't affected by the gun's change. It was probably just an effect of him overusing it in one night.

At least the incense had more room to disperse in the outside air. It bothered him less as he looked up at the stars, shut his eyes, and took a deep breath. The exhalation came out as a hoarse chuckle.

Brennan would want answers about how the night could have gone so wrong. That punk bitch would have bigger problems when Jacob saw him. Jacob wanted his whole operation. Guns, tricks, porn, drugs—hell, he'd even expand into gambling. Why not? He knew codes. He had imagination. He could certainly do better than those crooks operating in Atlantic City or Vegas. Shit, with his mind and this weapon from Heaven, he'd be running the entire region's underworld in no time. *Overlord of the underworld . . .* He chuckled again, louder.

"Must be some joke," he heard someone say.

"Care to share?" he heard a different voice say.

Jacob whirled around but saw no one. "Who—?"

Someone punched him in the face, a rapid right and left cross battered his cheeks, causing him to stumble backward and trip over a crouching body he couldn't see.

He cursed in pain and surprise on the way down. He managed to get up on a knee before he felt a boot kick him under his chin, forcing him down again.

HSA agents. Had to be. They were in some kind of armor that made them invisible.

Jacob stayed on his back as he reached for his piece. Someone stomped on his stomach. He hollered, balled up, and rolled to his side.

There were apparently two of them. One of them kicked him in the head and back while the other one spoke.

"We'd have preferred not to get involved. We usually just locate missing kids and lead the professional cleaners to the scum. We like to step back and let them do their job. But it looks like you found a toy. Guess we're force to play with you till the big guns arrive."

The voice wasn't a mature one. Sounded like a girl in her late teens or early twenties.

"Bitch," Jacob said, "I've got your big gun right here." He turned toward the one who was kicking him and thrust his whole body upward and forward. It seemed to surprise and knock the agent off balance, long enough for Jacob to draw his gun.

He pointed it toward the general direction of where he'd heard the voice and prepared to pull the trigger. The right side of his face exploded in searing pain, as if someone had hit him with a flaming bat.

He dropped the gun. Someone got him in a choke hold from behind. Jacob's knees buckled, allowing his attacker to tighten his hold even more. He could tell by the strength and aggressiveness exhibited that it was a male, but a young one.

Jacob used both arms to try to pry himself loose.

"You're not dealing with mere mortals anymore," the girl's voice said. "We can do things the likes of you couldn't possibly understand. Give up *now*."

He was more than tired of people telling him to lie down, stay put, and give up. He wasn't some bitch.

He kept his left hand on his assailant's arm while he stretched his right toward his gun. He tried to will it toward him.

Sheila shot out from nowhere, leaping and latching onto the invisible girl, who became visible when struck. All growl and tenacity, the bull terrier had gotten her by the throat. The girl flailed, trying at once to get the dog off and scramble away. But the bull terrier held on for dear life as it choke-bit out another's.

Jacob felt the choke hold loosen. He elbowed the guy behind him to get freer then reached out for his gun. In a second, it was in his hand. In another second, he whirled around and pulled the trigger.

He pegged it right. He pegged *him* right.

The kid flashed into sight when hit and immediately swelled up. He momentarily resembled a balloon figure made by a mad clown. And, when he popped, scattering his innards, Jacob laughed a hearty chuckle, even as a good portion landed on him.

He turned around to see Sheila still gnawing on the girl, who'd already begun a new existence as a corpse.

"Not mere mortals, huh?" he muttered. Yeah, they had a few tricks, but they looked and sounded like college students. Whatever they were, they hadn't a chance. His new appendage put him on equal footing with anything or anyone this planet shoved at him. *God's gun*—and he was the chosen one to wield it.

It now gave off a thicker smoke, a heavier scent, one that didn't disperse so easily. It lingered about him like a fog. But the piece still felt good in his hand. Like it never wanted to be released.

"Come at me, world!" he shouted. "I'm ready!"

Sheila burst into flames—flames that immediately snuffed out to leave a charred skeleton in their place.

Jacob froze.

"Sheila—?"

His little girl.

"*Sheila!*"

His body trembled uncontrollably.

"You said you were ready," a booming voice above him said. "I took you at your word."

Jacob looked up. Hovering several dozen feet in the air was a creature at least ten feet tall, if not more. Appearing mostly as a man, it was nude. Its body had a bodybuilder's physique. Its head was a unicorn's. Its hands appeared to be talons; its feet were cloven hooves. From the neck down, all of him—all of *it*—was clothed in rippled folds of multihued but transparent light.

"What the hell—?" Jacob whispered.

The creature slowly descended.

Jacob pointed the gun and pulled the trigger.

The creature continued its descent.

Jacob again pulled the trigger.

The creature was no more than ten feet from the ground.

Jacob concentrated now—on exploding bodies, scrambled entrails, broken limbs, ruptured organs—and pulled the trigger at each thought.

The creature stood in front of him and gazed down into his eyes.

"I believe you are finished," the creature thundered.

Jacob's knees buckled. But he refused to go down. He wouldn't cower.

"The fuck are you?" he asked.

"I am the Equinox. The magick you are wielding will not work on me. It has been born of an inferior art form."

Jacob didn't understand any of it. He only knew his little girl was dead, and his newest protector wasn't working in his time of greatest need.

His shoulders heaved as the corners of his eyes welled up. His voice cracked and wavered. "It's over, isn't it?"

"For you. Your world. Your kind. And your ideas." The creature stretched its right talon forward. The gun flew to it and hovered over as the creature moved its left talon on top of it. The gun crumpled in upon itself until pea sized, then winked out of sight.

Jacob looked up into those frightening, equine eyes. They were ablaze with a blue fury. The sight was dreadful enough, but Jacob wouldn't turn away. He wouldn't bend to his knees or beg. He fought back his tears. He swallowed until he was sure he'd sound like a man, not a coward. "What now? What are you going to do to me?"

"You?" the creature thundered. "I do not give a damn about you."

The folds of faint light enveloping the creature ruffled furiously until they appeared as a dozen pairs of far-reaching wings. Like a crossbow's bolt, the creature shot straight into the air and was out of sight—all in the time it took Jacob to gasp.

It wasn't wholly an expression of awe. His gasp unleashed the floodgates holding back what he'd felt for Sheila. He dropped to his knees.

His world . . . In one night, he'd experienced such power, had such dreams, and then . . .

No. Mourning would have to come later. He needed rest. He needed to figure out how to deal with Brennan.

It took more than one try, but he pushed himself up to his feet. His eyes welled at another glance at Sheila's remains. He then turned, took a deep breath, and trudged home. He'd return to bury her when he was stable enough to pay the proper respects.

Half a mile later, his patio in sight, he still had no idea of what to do or where to go when the sun rose. He couldn't return to the diner. Hell, even spending the night at his own pad was tempting fate. Maybe he'd hit the road, drive south.

He stepped onto the patio and looked down. Sheila's plastic bowl was full.

He stooped and looked closer. Hamburger, partially cooked but mostly pink. It being there was strange enough, but something else was funny with it.

He dipped two fingers in and brought them up to his nose. Two whiffs were all it took. Some kind of chemical—*poison*—had been mixed in. But not too much. Sheila's sense of smell would've picked it up, but she may have chowed down, ingesting everything before realizing it could do her harm. That was the probably the hope, anyway, of whoever put this here.

Jacob stood, wondering who possibly could have—

The blade penetrated several inches deep in his neck. It slid out like a finger from a glove before thrusting in and sliding out of another part of his neck.

With no words and hardly a thought, Jacob fell to the concrete, landing on his side. A hand grasped his shoulder and turned him to his back as the blade plunged into his chest.

The man on top of him moved erratically, and Jacob was fading out quickly. But through squinting eyes and blurred vision, he recognized the Ethiopian, mad as all hell, stabbing his chest and neck with a rarefied fury. He wouldn't stop anytime soon.

Jacob couldn't fight back. He only tried to chuckle at his final thought—that he'd soon resemble the meat in Sheila's bowl.

FOOLKILLERS

Avery Brocus should've used his real photo. He shouldn't have used his real name.

His fingers tapped the screen of his smartphone, lying flat on the table. A nervous tic. He wanted badly to text a buddy, asking him to run down and meet him at the wine bar. He needed a friend sitting at a nearby table, observing silently and ready to jump in if, instead of a young woman, some big bruiser showed up to blackmail or rob him.

Many thoughts breezed through as he waited for his kinda-sorta blind date to arrive, but the thought that he was being set up was like a tornado in his mind. He was almost dizzy with dread.

Avery wasn't entirely clear on what pushed him to set up a profile on the Freakfinder site. Curiosity was certainly a factor. He'd been hearing about hook-up websites for years, and Freakfinder was the one that promised the most success (or your money back). Loneliness wasn't the issue. Sober or tipsy he always swore he was—and *felt* he was—happy living alone with two cats. While setting up his profile, he'd muttered something to himself about satisfying an urge, scratching an itch that was more irritating than mere curiosity.

In seventeen years of legal adulthood, he'd never had a relationship last more than six weeks. He never found his dates wholly appealing. Oftentimes the feeling was more than mutual. Sometimes he'd try to stick with a woman that shared similar interests since, the older he got, the more uncomfortable he felt going to dinner or attending a show alone. But no matter how many shared interests, after a while the woman's presence began to grate, the phone calls and texting became a nuisance, and the meet-ups a chore akin to cleaning the bathroom after a week of neglect. He went on hiatus to concentrate on his job and to figure himself out. After about a year, he had an epiphany: he wasn't attracted to women his own age. He just plain didn't like what his generation was into, what they talked about, their hang-outs or their hang-ups. He wasn't a man of his time. He wanted difference. He wanted exoticism. He had a *fetish*.

In second grade, he once had a substitute teacher named Ms. Lovelace. Blonde, blue eyes, long legs, and curvy in all the right places. He couldn't believe her name or her looks, but he believed that's when it all started, his yearning for older women—women at least fifteen years older than he. Beyond taboo, he'd more than an inkling that this was perverse. He tried to suppress it, but the inclination stayed with him through high school and college. Older women turned his head and held his attention several seconds longer than the women in his peer group.

In his early thirties, when he was finally ready to give up and admit it to himself (if no one else), he started to indulge a little. He began scouring the web and watching MILF porn at midnight before crawling into bed at two a.m. A month later he graduated to hot-and-frisky granny porn. After two years of watching this stuff almost every night, he couldn't take it anymore. He wanted the real thing.

One night, after two glasses of Pinot, rather than clicking on his favorite porn site, he searched for hook-up sites catering to those who wanted to explore beyond their own age range. His profile was nothing special, though he made sure the first sentence highlighted the fact he was drug-, disease-, and drama-free. His username was PurplePet8er—a twist on a second-grader's joke. He posted pictures of a physique sculpted by five hundred push-ups a day. The pics were all nude, but they didn't venture below the waist or higher than the chin.

Over the course of two months, he clicked "like" on several dozen profiles, received one half-hearted response for every eight emails he sent, and added about a dozen reasonably attractive divorcees and attached-but-looking cougars to his hotlist. Then, he saw her profile. She wasn't in his preferred range, but those eyes . . . that face . . . Both seemed to glow. She was twenty-two, thirteen years his junior, and judging by her detailed profile, she seemed far more sexually experienced than he was sure he ever wanted to be. But he sent her a "wink." The next night he added her to his hotlist. The following night, an email: *You're beautiful. I'd wish I'd met you in another life.* The following night, he received an email: *What's wrong with this one?*

A conversation started. Sentences were volleyed before paragraphs were carefully composed and exchanged. One night, after four glasses of Pinot, when he was about to hit "send" on a 3,000 word email, he deleted it and sent two words instead. *Wanna meet?*

Yes, of course. But send me a face pic first, and tell me your name :)

He'd panicked. His body reflected the efforts of a gym rat, while his face looked like it had been bitten by rats. Blemishes from mild but incurable acne and unhealed scars resulting from one too many shaving cuts didn't make for a pretty picture. He wasn't about to run out and buy a makeup kit; at the time it made far more sense to send her someone else's face. He found something suitable on an obscure site show-casing the photos of young and obscure literary authors. He was so giddy with the find that he didn't think to make up a name. It was only when sobriety kicked in the next morning that he realized he'd gotten it backward. She was going to see exactly what he looked like when they met, but he could've kept his real name hidden for weeks, months, or even longer. Just stupid.

And now he was stuck—stuck in a cozy wine bar. It had the capacity to seat twenty-five in the main area. It was currently seating fifteen. Avery had arrived at 3:00, thirty minutes earlier than the agreed upon meeting time, and certainly early enough to get a choice seat in the dimly lit back, facing the front door, blinking at the sunlight each time someone entered in silhouette.

Then she entered. He didn't blink. The sunlight that had shadowed all other entrants seemed to clothe her. The normally banal pink tank top and blue jeans shone like the raiment of a fairy tale princess on her. Her face glowed like a vanilla sun, just like in her picture. And her smile was straight out of a toothpaste commercial. He must've been drunk on wine fumes.

She made eye contact the moment she stepped over the threshold. Hers—implausibly—twinkled. The smile neither left her face nor changed its contours as she made her way to the table.

"Avery?"

He stood, knees wobbling as much as the three-legged table. "Charity?"

She nodded. Beauty *and* brains. Not only was she a five-foot-five bundle of hotness, she was also smart enough not to give her real name.

Avery extended his hand. She waved it away and moved in for a hug.

Disengaging from the tangle, she said, "Never worry, it *is* my real name." She winked, then took her seat and picked up the menu. "So what should we wet our tongues with first?"

Avery remained standing, unsteady. This girl, this beautiful girl, had eased into his presence as comfortably as if she'd been dating him for a year.

"Uh, there's an Oregon Pinot that's good," he said, finding his seat, not once taking his eyes off her. "It's from the Willamette Valley. Best Pinot in the New World."

"Well, far be it from me to resist the best of anything, from any world."

She peered at him over the menu. Avery was half expecting her to wink again—wink one of those twinkling eyes—but instead hers simply met his, unblinking, warming him. He flinched and looked away, resting his eyes on the table as she laid the menu down.

"You looking to call for backup?" she asked.

Avery met her eyes again, only to see hers focused on the screen of his cell. While waiting for her arrival, he'd pulled up the Freakfinder site, intending to locate and re-read her profile before meeting her. But his phone displayed the site's homepage, with its dozen squares of x-rated photos posted by shameless women.

Avery snatched the phone and jammed it into his jeans pocket. "I just wanted to remember what you looked like, so I could recognize you when you walked in."

"Well, I don't look like a vagina. And that's all I saw on your screen."

She grinned as she said it. Avery tried to chuckle in response, but it sounded more as if he were coming down with a cold than sharing a laugh.

"Besides," she said, "all I have on my profile are head shots. The number of times we've communicated, I would hope you'd have me memorized by now. You, on the other hand, were a mystery—until the last minute."

"Yeah," Avery shrugged and signaled for the waiter, "about my face pic—"

"I knew it was a fake the second I got it. Figured the body

photos were, too—our little hug just now told me that they weren't. Honestly, before I came through the door, I was fully expecting to meet a woman. I just knew the name wasn't fake."

She'd said it all with a smile, not a smirk. Nevertheless, Avery couldn't help but feel embarrassed. His eyes began to drift toward the tabletop again . . . He had to shake it off. This was a once-in-a-lifetime opportunity. He had to choke back his nervousness and exude confidence. Not fake it—*believe* it.

His eyes met hers as he straightened his back. "Avery is a fake name. My real one is Chastity."

Her expression twitched as the aura around her face seemed to flicker. Avery sensed she didn't immediately get the joke. He was relieved enough when she laughed seconds later, though he was still questioning his eyesight.

They ordered their wine, and then Charity said, "Well, whoever said anyone on the net has to be who they say they are? The unwritten law is to be something completely different from reality."

"Funny thing that your name really is Charity . . . Right?"

She gave him a slow nod.

"Because, you agreeing to meet me," he said, "meet me openly and *honestly*, seems to be an act of kindness. We're from such different worlds."

"In a manner of speaking, yes. But we're not totally different. Trying to live up to the name my makers gave me, I use my spare time trying to help the unfortunate. Not too different from the volunteer work you said you do with children . . . but, then, most men on those sites claim they're athletic, kind, and attentive, with a generous sense of humor and an inclination to help others."

"Guilty of the same," Avery said, giving her his first broad smile. "And I have the evidence to prove it."

They drank, traded anecdotes, alternated bathroom breaks, and shared laughs for two hours. Avery then paid the check and escorted Charity outside.

"Can I see you again?" he asked.

"If you remember to call me, you can."

They hugged less awkwardly than before and went their separate ways. Avery walked five blocks, sobering slightly, before reaching his Honda. It had a yellow slip of paper under the wiper. He'd only put enough money in the meter for one hour, the limit. If he'd known he and Charity would hit it off so well, he would've parked in a garage.

He put the ticket in his pocket and sped home, not even caring if he was pulled over and slapped with a DUI. This had been one of the best afternoons of his life, and there was little he could think of that would ruin it.

He parked on the street, a block away from his apartment building's lot. He wanted to walk a bit more to clear his head, still in a haze from wine and thoughts of a long-term future with Charity.

He reached into his pocket for the receipt, wanting to look at the number she had scribbled on the back of it, just to make sure it was real. The receipt was there; the parking ticket was there; his smartphone was gone. He must've left it back at the bar. As fortune would have it, he'd gotten rid of his landline a year ago, so he had no way to call and ask. He decided to feed the cats, have a big glass of water, then head on back.

He pushed the button on his key to shut off the apartment's alarm. Opening the door, he almost fell backward when a pungent odor plugged his nostrils.

Avery coughed. "Sara? Cara?"

The cats didn't come when he called. Incurably shy, they always hid from strangers, running under the couch or bed whenever they heard a voice other than his. But they always came mewing when he was alone. He checked the kitchen, then under the couch. It was a one bedroom apartment, so they couldn't have gone far. He hurried into the bedroom to check under the bed. He didn't need to.

The carcasses were lying on the bed, headless and split open down the middle, their entrails removed and scattered across the bedspread. Taken together, it seemed to form some sort of pattern. Avery didn't know what, but he immediately guessed it was satanic.

He didn't have to guess much when he looked at his laptop. The cats' heads were on either side, dead-staring back at him. Whoever did this had turned the laptop on and logged into his account on Freakfinder. He stared at his profile page. It had been updated to include pictures of his face, details about his home life, and even more details about his work life. The last sentence of the About You section read: "And I kill kittens."

No telling how many subscribers to the site had seen it, but one was more than enough. Avery ignored the blood smeared on his keyboard as he hurried to delete everything. He then bolted out of his apartment for his car. While running, he tried to figure which was closer, the police station or the wine bar. Should he get his phone first, or get the cops?

Someone was leaning against his Civic. *Charity.* She wore the same smile that had dazzled him earlier, but it didn't invoke the same feelings as before. Coming from the shock in his apartment to the shock of seeing her appear from nowhere made him more nauseous than anything.

"What are you doing—?" he began.

She held up his smartphone. "You forgot this."

He didn't know where to begin. She seemed to pick up the hint.

"After we said our temporary goodbyes, I went back to the bar to ask for the name of one of the wines we had. They told me they found your phone under our table." She handed it to him. "It must've slid out of your pocket at some point."

"How did you know where I lived?"

She cocked her head. "I have your phone. You never turned it off. It was pretty easy to find your provider account info. Nothing you have on there is password protected. Not smart."

Avery switched the cell to the phone function and began dialing. "I have to call the police."

"Hey"—Charity held up her hands—"I didn't look at that much. It's not like I hacked into your bank account."

"No, someone broke into my place, and— Hello? 911? I— *Dammit*, they put me on hold!"

"Don't you have a house alarm? Why don't you just set it off? It'll probably get the cops here faster."

"Yeah, good idea." Avery hung up and turned to run back home. "I'll see you later."

It was much later when he realized there were probably better ideas, like staying on the line. But thinking straight had been a problem for him all day. Only that night, after the cops left, did he wonder how much digging Charity had actually done on his cell phone, and why she seemed so positive his apartment had an alarm—an alarm whose deactivation code was stored in his phone's list of computer and email passwords.

MONDAY at the office began the way of all Monday mornings, with a surly mood permeating the air, one that would only begin to dissipate once everyone had gotten halfway through their first cup of coffee. Avery and most of his fellow middle managers were already on their second cups. He anticipated he'd be on his fourth by the time someone from the police department called to let him know how the investigation was going. It was a new—and ironic—department policy: all victims were required to be notified of their case's status within twenty-four hours, whether or not there'd been any progress. After that, it was the victim's responsibility to follow up. Avery considered it ironic due to the open secret of how leisurely the department operated.

He'd gotten little sleep. It wasn't just that he slept on the stiff leather couch (there was no way in hell he was going anywhere near the bed), but he couldn't stop thinking about potential culprits. Who were his enemies? Who hated him so much that they'd break into his house and not steal or break anything but kill his closest companions and try to ruin his reputation? What the hell had he ever done to anyone?

He moved the cursor to open an email that popped into his inbox, then his screen went black. Seconds later it came to back to life, showing his Freakfinder profile page bright as day. Avery panicked as he heard others around him gasping. He quickly looked over both shoulders. No one was peering through the entranceway to his cubicle; none of his neighbors were peering through the walls, staring at his screen.

Middle manager status notwithstanding, he and everyone else who did work of middling relevance sat within the labyrinth of cubicles that covered most of the football-field-sized floor. Only the top dogs got the offices lining the walls, while the lower levels got a seat on the long tables in the center of the room. But no one remained hidden. Glass and mostly transparent plastic composed the office and cubicle walls. Part of the trends of the decade: shorter buildings, bigger floors, and transparency. And nosier coworkers.

Avery thought—hoped, *prayed*—he'd imagined the gasps and subsequent chatter. Or, if real, that it was due to something he wasn't seeing. What he was seeing now was having the jittering effect of ten coffees, particularly since the profile was the doctored page he thought he'd deleted.

Then as now, he banged away at his keyboard, trying to get the image off his screen before anyone saw. Nothing worked. He could scroll up and down, taking in all the pictures, all the lurid prose describing his dreams and desires and proclivities, but he couldn't click away from the page. He couldn't even reduce its size. As he prepared to jam his finger into the power button, the screen went blank. Seconds later, he was staring at his work email again.

No gasps from him or anyone else this time, just his own heavy sigh of relief. He prepared to open the email that had popped into his inbox a few minutes ago when he noticed a new one. Subject line: Ready to meet your new Match? Sender: Adult Freakfinder.

Shit. He received such messages through a personal email account he'd set up for this very purpose. When trying to delete his account on Sunday, had he mistakenly typed in his work email address?

He deleted the message unread and picked up his desk phone. He needed a distraction. He needed to take his eyes off his computer for a few minutes. He called the police department's non-emergency number and was put on hold, then bounced around for five minutes, until he was finally transferred to someone who could give him an update.

"We were going to call you this afternoon."

"I know," Avery said, "but I just couldn't wait."

"Well, we have news, but it's nothing that's going to reassure you."

Avery sighed. "Of course. Nothing about the last twenty-four hours has been reassuring."

"There was no forced entry into your place. No fingerprints anywhere, other than yours. And out of the people we've been able to talk to so far, none of them saw anything or anyone suspicious around your building."

The officer didn't say it, but Avery got the implication. So far, he was the only suspect in the slaughter of his cats and the attempt to ruin his reputation.

"If you want any additional updates," the officer said. "Please come down to the station and ask in person."

Of course.

Avery hung up as an announcement came over the intercom,

booming through the warehouse-sized room. "Mr. Avery Brocus, a Mr. Charity Mansion is here to see you. Please come to the reception area."

Avery shook his head. *Charity*? Was "Mansion" her last name? And what was up with the "mister"? He couldn't have heard all of that right. His ears had to be deceiving him; but his eyes . . .

His cubicle—maybe luckily, maybe not—wasn't that far from the reception area. His knees wobbled like gelatin as he slowly stood, peering over the cubicle wall. Many others around him were doing the same. Something in the pit of his stomach told him what to expect. But after his eyes scanned and met those of the visitor, the dreadful feeling in his stomach dropped lower, inciting nausea.

The tall man seemed to be in his mid- to late fifties—it was hard to tell as he clearly spent a lot of time in the sun, undoubtedly on a Harley. His orangish skin and biker jacket weren't the only giveaways. The shades, bandana, and white horseshoe mustache completed the look. The man was beefy, and he stood in a manner suggesting he was concealing something in his jacket, something long and made of metal.

This was some sick joke. His coworkers certainly thought so, doing little to conceal their snickers and chortles as Avery shuffled through the labyrinth toward the reception area. He considered running off in a different direction, but he couldn't think of a safe destination.

"Hello, Mr. Brocus." The biker's voice was as raspy as Avery had assumed.

Avery stammered and coughed once before asking, "Can I help you?"

"You've already started," the biker said with a sneer. "You agreed to make a donation to Charity, Brocus. And I will have Mercy on your soul when it is complete."

Avery shook his head. "I'm afraid I don't—"

"Excuse me for attempting to be polite for the sake of the

ladies"—he nodded toward the four middle-aged receptionists occupying one long desk—"but I was talking about my wife, you little fucker."

Avery swallowed and tried to steady his knees and his voice. "Sir, this is a place of business."

"Yes," he said with a growl, "and I'm here to discuss you sticking yours into mine."

All four receptionists regarded the two men with expressions of stark horror. Avery felt like they looked but tried to keep a brave face as he said, "Maybe we'd better talk at my desk."

"Yeah." The biker nodded and turned toward the cubicle maze as Avery read the stitchwork on the back of his jacket: Hell's Mercy. He sure hoped for mercy as he led the potential neck-breaker toward his desk.

This was Charity's husband? The pairing made no sense. Even if true, was this guy so jealous that he'd threaten or beat Avery just for having wine with the woman? *That* made a little more sense. If he looked like this guy and was able to pull a woman like Charity, he would jealously guard her too.

But Avery *had* a woman like Charity. At least, he was on the verge of getting her. Why couldn't *he* be the one to jealously guard her? She was special enough to fight for. In the brief amount of time he'd spent with her, she'd made him feel like a new man, reinvigorated; his desire for older women had been wiped away by one much younger woman. His thing for older women may've been sourced from a deep down desire to be taught in some secret, beautiful, pleasure that only an older, wiser woman could give him. That was a childish fantasy. A *perverse* fantasy. But his interest in Charity seemed more natural, more correct, something he wouldn't have to hide. Modern society would tolerate an older man with a younger woman. Nod at, smile at, and applaud it.

But to keep a woman like her—a once-in-a-lifetime opportunity—he'd have to shake this bruiser off. He'd again have choke back his nervousness and exude confidence. Not fake it—*believe* it. And then do something with it.

He steered the biker around twists and turns easily navigable only by long-term employees. Avery was no longer headed toward his little space but toward the grander area in the middle, where all the lower level employees sat at the long tables working on their tablets and laptops. If anything happened, security personnel could respond to this area quicker. There were four routes that cut directly through the maze.

Avery stopped and tried staring through the man's shades. "Whatever we have to discuss, we might as well discuss it here."

The biker looked around, meeting the glances of the curious employees who quickly pretended they found their work more interesting than him.

"Okay, pal. Looks like I've got you right where I want you."

"Listen. Charity and I only—"

"Charity and *I*, we make something of a wonderful team, see." He removed his shades. "We specialize in giving people, not what they want, but what they really need."

The man had no irises, no pupils. Black marbles with golden swirls filled his eyesockets.

Avery stepped backward. "What the fuck are you?"

"A philosopher." He smiled the same smile Charity had a day before. "One who has studied and examined your kind. Inside and out. Look around you. Look at where you've chosen to spend the majority of your waking hours. An illusion of order—similar clothing, identical workspaces, the caste levels . . . And at the same time, an illusion of disorder—a maze filled with messy work stations, hungover office drones overqualified for their meaningless activities . . ."

A philosopher, maybe. Typical biker, certainly not. Avery couldn't help but look the man in the eyes as he responded; he was less scared than in awe. "I just work here. I had nothing to do with setting anything, *any* of this up. And what does this have to do with Charity?"

The biker smirked. "Swimming in illusions, and dying of thirst. Your kind is *wanting*, man. You offered yourself to Charity, so I'm offering you Mercy."

He raised both arms above his head and snapped his fingers. The lights and computers blinked. An orange haze tinged the air while, on each nearby laptop screen, Avery saw photoshopped pictures of him in a variety of compromising situations and positions with old women and young boys. Each screen held a lurid picture for a few seconds before flashing to another regrettable one.

The office was in an uproar. The images were apparently on every screen. Many people screamed about lost work; the rest screamed about the disgusting images flashing before their eyes.

"Wh— Stop! Why are you doing this? *How* are you doing this? *Stop* it!" Avery's pleas and questions were met with a grin as the biker's sunbaked face paled and emitted a faint glow that steadily grew brighter.

"Your nervous system," the biker said, "the human nervous system imposed all these illusions of Order and Disorder on the universe—but illusions aren't true. An objective perspective of the truth can only be obtained by giving to Charity and accepting Mercy."

It was only then that Avery realized the biker was referring to himself as Mercy. And it was then, amid the pandemonium, that he saw all of his coworkers looking at him, switching their gazes between him and their computer screens, screaming out of disgust, screaming about lost documents, hollering insults. Even the big shots were coming out of their offices and making their own vocal contributions to the madness.

Avery turned for the nearest exit, but the biker's arm shot forward like a frog's tongue; his hand around Avery's throat was just as sticky. Avery was forced to look into those gold-streaked eyes as the biker challenged him.

"This is the *crux* of giving and receiving. Those who've been abused by the images, the ordered and disordered details of your life, they're limited to the people in this wide, wide room. I've blocked the exits. Only these people know your secrets, true and false. So you, in your heightened state of anxiety, have a choice. Shall I kill them and let only you go? Or shall I let all of you live with what you've all seen?"

The biker was correct—Avery was now more nervous, more *scared* than he'd ever been. The choice at first seemed a ridiculous one, until he repeated it to himself for the fifth time. In neither case would this, this *Mercy*, kill his body. It was a choice between the death of his conscience and morals, by ordering all his coworkers dead, or the death of his reputation and ultimately —*probably*—his sanity, wondering at all times what all these people, former friends and acquaintances, might be thinking about him.

"You have five seconds."

Five seconds before what? Which choice would this tiger-eyed psychotic take? Avery couldn't risk staying silent. He'd make his own choice.

"Kill m—"

The biker choked the remainder away. "Time's up," he smirked. "And I heard: kill *many*." He released his hold.

Before Avery could regain his breath, let alone speak a word of protest, the biker darted at three or four times the speed of a tiger into the labyrinth of cubicles, snatching each man or woman within reach and, with blinding speed, thrusting his hands into their backs, lighting up their bodies and ripping out their spines before moving on to the next one.

Avery was too frightened to run anywhere. The biker, the *whatever*, was moving faster and faster as he went—running and ripping, lighting up bodies as if they were lamps before unplugging them. There was no escape for Avery or anyone else. He would just have to wait where he was, waiting to meet his fate after all the others.

He had a hard time making sense of any of the past twenty-four hours' happenings. As everyone else ran around screaming, he numbly watched Mercy darting through the labyrinth like a grotesque version of the fabled and already grotesque Minotaur. He just as numbly turned his eyes upward to see the ripple in the air near the ceiling, several dozen feet up, and the violet man-sized eagle materializing through it like stained light through a closed window.

The sight of an eagle comprised of violet flames was only in his view for a few seconds before it entered the labyrinth like a bundle of hopping sparks, evading every living person until meeting Mercy head on. The violet bird then flared, shooting itself out of the maze and into the air above Avery, close to the area where it had initially appeared. Two flaming talons held Mercy by his arms, but the one-time biker had no time to either struggle or say a word before the bird flipped him and flung him down. Mercy crashed through a table adjacent to Avery's, hollering as any mortal would after being thrown with enough force to break wood two inches thick.

Mercy was immobilized, done for. But that didn't stop the violet bird of light from swooping down to snatch him by the throat and lift him out of the debris.

Avery watched the giant bird shift its form, resolving itself into something with human-like arms and legs. The spanning wings of violet light remained as the beak shifted to a helmet's position on a head appearing more wolf-like than anything. The eight-foot being pulled the marble-eyed biker within a few inches of its canine snout.

"I have mercy on your soul." The creature of light spoke with a voice enveloped in thunder before streams of light shot from its head into the biker's eyes, ears, nostrils, and mouth. The biker's skin turned cloud-white with graying spots as it sunk in on itself. The streams of light seemed to act as proboscises, shifting through various hues of red as they sucked the life out of the biker, withering his skin until it appeared as an ash-colored raisin. Finished, the violet creature dropped the corpse back into the mess of splintered wood and broken laptops and turned toward Avery.

"Where's the other one?"

The rumbling voice didn't stifle all the screaming and terrified expressions, but it quieted the room. Or maybe Avery was so tuned in to this wondrous being addressing him that his attention hadn't much for anyone else around him. He was also speechless. The violet being was impatient.

It stepped toward Avery, shifting its appearance again, wiping away the violet flames covering its visage, shape-shifting its face into that of a man with vanilla-violet skin and deep purple eyes. Its body remained robed in ruffles of light that, in such close proximity, Avery now knew was simply *light*—though maybe not *simply*, but definitely not flames, despite the appearance. The only warmth Avery felt was from his own nervousness, nervousness preventing him from fleeing as well as speaking, a nervousness anyone would feel when addressed by an eight-foot-tall angel.

"Avery Brocus," the angel said, "where is the other one?"

"I— Other—?"

The angel closed the distance, standing no more than a few feet in front of Avery. Avery swallowed as he looked into those soul-sucking eyes.

"What is happening?"

"You opened a line of communication with demons," the angel said. "They were beginning a ritual, using you as the focal point."

"This . . . guy? A demon?"

"I have another word for his kind, but 'demon' is the apt term for your understanding. They work in pairs. They present themselves as artists or philosophers, walking works of beauty or fascination. In reality, they make fools of their subjects; they then kill the bodies and extinguish the souls of those connected to the fool, as many as possible at one time."

Avery nodded. "So I'm the fool." He should've known someone like Charity wouldn't be interested in him as a man, or even as a human being. He'd been scammed by someone out to bruise his psyche and rob him of his very core.

"Their minds and souls were shaped in another dimension," the angel said. "Their philosophies and art are incomprehensible to those in your realm. Each pair of demons has unique methods, but these two targeted men and women looking for *love*, then psychologically tormented them in a compressed amount of time in order to feed off of their psychic energy. Heightened anxiety, fear, embarrassment, and confusion, all of it released with a psychic deathscream, satiates them."

"And, you," Avery said. "You're a guardian angel? Out to protect me and the other fools?"

"I am Valentinus. I am out to correct errors and save the chosen for the Hereafter."

Avery shook his head. "It's like something out of the Book of Revelation."

"No," Valentinus said. "A new book is being written about The End. About *now*."

Avery's eyes dropped to the floor. Today was his own personal Judgment Day—and what a life . . . What a fucking life he'd led. He'd trudged through school, got a boring job, and took even less interesting vacations. And then, after—he *thought*—finally getting in touch with himself, he set out on a curving road to satisfy an admittedly odd craving; detoured, he opened a gate leading to Hell. The punishment didn't fit the crime. But, what *was* the crime?

"What now?" he asked.

"I must deal with the damaged souls here," Valentinus said. "But I must deal with the other demon afterward. Go out and find her. *Hold* her. I am sure she will hone in on you."

Valentinus leapt into the air and hovered near the ceiling. Avery was half expecting to see a patch of air rippling near the angel. Instead, the rippling patch appeared near Avery, off to his right. A portal, he surmised, that would get him out of here. He stepped toward it, then paused to look at Valentinus as the angel flared, sending out innumerable streamers of violet light. He saw the light piercing the faces of his nearby colleagues. They didn't scream, but their bodies were rapidly transfigured, twisting like pretzels in the making. Not wanting to be next, Avery ran into the portal.

THE PORTAL DEPOSITED Avery on the steps outside the police station. He was surprised it worked as he'd wished it would, but shocked the portal didn't place him right outside his workplace. When running through the tear in the air, he'd thought of running to the police. Something had read his mind and made the task easy by not forcing him to run. The difficulty was in trying to talk to the police. They rolled their eyes at the mention of demons and angels. It was only after they demanded he leave the station or be locked up that he realized he should've simply said that his coworkers were under attack; he shouldn't have jammed that statement at the end of one confirming the existence of the inhabitants of Heaven and Hell on Earth.

He trudged home, taking the time halfway to make a 911 call on his smartphone. *Workplace massacre—please hurry.* Whatever happened next, happened.

When it was within sight, he headed toward one of his building's side entrances, the one closest to his apartment. Charity was leaning against a nearby tree. Seeing her in skimpy blue jean shorts and a pink crop top, an outfit cut and created out of her previous one, Avery almost began to feel for her all over again. He truly was a fool.

"Why?" he asked when within non-shouting distance.

She straightened. Appearing genuinely confused, she looked in his eyes. "Why what?"

"Why did I have to be the one to let this loose?"

He knew he shouldn't have said it. He should've acted like nothing was wrong. He should've smiled and waved upon seeing her, suggested they walk to the nearest coffee shop, and there he'd keep her until Valentinus arrived. But in her presence, his pride overwhelmed good sense.

"What are you talking about?" Charity asked.

"You." He gazed hard into her blue-shimmering eyes as his brow furrowed. "Demons."

"Oh." She turned away, toward the shrubbery. "He came."

"Yes," Avery said. "Your so-called husband came and ripped apart my coworkers."

"What?" She again looked into his eyes; hers seemed to be on the edge of fury. "Valentinus is *not* my husband!"

Avery shook his head. "No—*Mercy*—the biker! The philoso— You *know* who I'm talking about!"

"He's Valentinus's herald," Charity said. "He appears before Valentinus. He breaks up bodies—physically and psychically—so Valentinus can suck out the souls."

Avery gaped at her. He didn't know what to say. He'd been shoved into a battle between angels and demons and wasn't sure which was which. Everything he'd witnessed over the past several hours had been unbelievable before being plausibly explained by the violet angel. But now, what Charity was saying, coupled with what he'd seen the violet one do . . . Valentinus could just have easily been the real evildoer.

"I'll be honest with you," Charity said. "I found you online and established contact because I knew Valentinus was zeroing in on you, following your electronic movements. He's a demon that feeds on those who make 'errors' in love; those who don't stick to what is true and proper. I was hoping to reach out to you in time, to protect you. When I went through your phone yesterday, I was trying to find a way to trace and locate him while he was spying on you from another dimension. I wasn't successful."

"But— Why did you kill my cats?"

"I didn't kill your cats, Avery. If anyone did, it was Mercy, setting up the beginning of a ritual feast for him and Valentinus."

"Why should I believe you?"

"Look at me." Her eyes twinkled as they had on Sunday. It wasn't a trick on his eyes. She wasn't fully human. "Avery, *I* am the angel. *They* are the demons. Weigh our appearances. Think about the fate of your coworkers."

They were probably all dead, snuffed away to oblivion. Avery was the sole survivor, living his life, the life he always lived— going along only to be tricked in one direction then kicked in another. A fool.

"I came here to see how you were, waiting till you got off work. I should've come by this morning. But you're alive, and Valentinus will be coming to finish what he started. Here." She reached into her shorts pocket and pulled out a ring with a large mounted diamond. It had to be worth a small fortune. She handed it to him. "Put this on your finger. I'm limited in what I can do against him. I may not be able to beat him. At most, I will probably distract him. If I do, *punch* him. Thrust the diamond into his eye. It will extinguish him."

Avery looked at the ring, wondering. He was about to ask her why she didn't wear it when nerves scratched at the back of his neck. He instinctively looked up to see the air shimmering just above the top of the tree. Valentinus appeared like before, a giant eagle composed of violet fire, but he readily shifted into an angelic posture as he descended, landing on the grass a couple dozen feet away from them.

"Your time is up, Errorist," he thundered. "Your partner has been subdued. Much of your power is gone."

Charity looked at Valentinus warily, then at Avery. Her eyes twinkled as she grabbed him by the shoulders, pulled, and gave him a passionate kiss. She pulled away and whispered, "I'm sorry you were caught up in this."

Valentinus approached. "Never again."

Charity looked at him, more resolved, and stepped forward. "You're forgetting—"

"I have forgotten nothing," he thundered.

"You're forgetting," Charity repeated, "*you* made me."

"In another lifetime," Valentinus said. "I made a mistake. I'm correcting it now."

Charity pointed at him, her arms like rifles. Or maybe more like leaf blowers. Somehow she blew away much of the violet light enveloping Valentinus, making him appear as a mere giant of a man, naked, with a violet-tinged vanilla hue.

She glanced at Avery. "Remember—"

Valentinus darted in and grabbed her by the forearms. Charity hardly had time to look him in the face before he snapped her arms like matchsticks. The woman loosed an unearthly scream that Avery was sure would be heard blocks away, maybe even all the way to the police station.

But no one was coming to the rescue. Time was crucial. Mercy had given him a choice between two options; he'd tried to choose a third, and it didn't turn out so well. Charity didn't really give him an explicit choice, but . . . Each man and woman would have a personal Judgment Day—compressed chaos, and a *split second* to make a final decision.

Avery ran at the two and lunged. Before either could flinch, he punched the jewel into the eye.

Charity fell backward onto the grass, grinning without sound, until her mouth froze into a wide smile displaying off-white teeth.

"Why did you do that?"

Avery looked up, into the otherworldly purple irises of Valentinus.

"I did as she asked," Avery said. "*Remembered*. All that she'd said. She was full of contradictions. Inconsistencies. She was a classic scammer. All the time I was with her I was nervous, anxious, and she was feeding off of it. I didn't fully trust her."

"And yet you did exactly what she wanted you to do."

Avery shook his head. "She wanted me to do this—*that* —to you."

Valentinus looked at the ring on Avery's finger. "That wouldn't have hurt me." He held up his left hand; a diamond and gold ouroboros twisted around the angel's middle and ring fingers. "She knew it would have no effect on me or else she would've done it herself. What you've done is extinguish her soul, preventing me from taking it."

Avery stared at the diamond ring on his own finger. *Fool. Scammed again. How many more times?*

"Her soul has dissipated in a fashion that makes it impossible to recollect." Valentinus looked at Avery as he reassumed his robes of ruffling light. "I needed to pair her soul with her partner's."

"Why?" Avery stepped forward, curiosity overwhelming his fear. "*Why?*"

"Books are being written. Plots are being tilled. A harmonious Hereafter is not a foregone conclusion." He turned his piercing eyes to Avery.

Avery recoiled at a realization. "No . . . No *way!*"

"You accepted her ring, and her kiss. You must reap what you sow."

"But— But I never really had a choice! Not a fair one!"

"You make a choice each time you take a breath, even if you believe it's involuntary."

"Fine," Avery shouted, "then I'm telling you with all the breath I have left that I refuse to let you take me!"

"You are out of choices."

Avery lowered his head, shaking it. "Not fair . . ."

"That's always been the way of life. Its end rushes at you. A minor sin overwhelms you, buries you, sends you to where you don't think you deserve to go, because you've really done nothing . . . But now, there's me. I offer redemption. Your life won't be quick, dirty, and meaningless. I am giving you a chance to take part in a minor plot to save a world."

Avery raised his head. He hadn't completely lost the will to protest, but he was losing it, along with the slivers of skin he felt being peeled from him like an onion as he wept, gazing into those eyes, striped violet and gold, unspooling . . . The angel's gaze made Avery more cognizant of something within himself, something deep within, something the remaining fragments of his here-and-now consciousness could only describe as a glob of honey. His *soul*. Avery was being stripped down to his bare essence, a realization that struck him before the angel's eyes flashed and he felt memories—every memory of every second of his life—flash-flooding through him before his very heart was snatched out and his consciousness blacked out.

THE ROUTINE BEGAN like it always began—without beginning. There was no day or night in the vineyard maze, only chores to perform, another dimension's soil to cultivate. As near as Avery could tell, thousands of souls were working on this one plot. His soul and that of the one once known as Mercy worked together. All souls were required to pair up. And Mercy, reformed as he had been, was an ideal partner.

Here, Avery's once deep-down desire had been mostly fulfilled. As they worked, he and the other souls were taught pleasing, beautiful secrets that only something much wiser than any human of any known gender or age could give him. It was no childish fantasy; it was a ripening and wonderful reality. A new world was coming.

Presently, he paused his work to gaze upward. The immobile thousand-foot-tall giant at whose feet he worked had the body of a human woman. Never mind there were no actual humans in this realm—there were only angels, their enemies, and once-human souls. Inside the giant's head were angels, guiding, making schemes and preparations to ensure they and their chosen ones survived the erasure of Earth and its universe. The angels were trusted completely. No soul under them would even consider doubting their devices.

In the labyrinthine vineyard of unearthly delights, Avery was happy to be a slave, a stripped-naked soul. There was so much that would not be understood until after the final Revelation unfolded, ushering in the Hereafter, but he was secure in the knowledge he'd never again be anyone's—or anything's—*fool*.

KNOTTY & ICE

Neal didn't stop for the cyclist. He didn't even take the time to consider himself lucky when the kid swerved out of his Acura's path.

On a mission, he took up two spaces in the parking lot then almost forgot to lock the car's doors as he dashed for the convenience store's entrance. He hustled up and down the aisles twice before finally losing it.

"*Dammit*—Don't you have any Listerine?"

"Sorry, shiny," the clerk hollered back at him.

Neal knew his skin was still covered in baby oil—only in the car did he realize it might've been wise to rinse off before he'd left Lady Kat's room—but the fact the clerk could tell he was slicked up from a couple dozen feet away only made him more anxious. What if the chuckling fool made a leap in logic and figured it out? Shiny head and arms sticking out of a wrinkled, stained polo . . . Couldn't have been the worst or oddest of what has passed through the convenience store; but the clerk wouldn't take his eyes off him.

"We have a dry mouth oral rinse." The fool, still chuckling, may or may not have been trying to be helpful.

"I need something that kills odors," Neal said. "*Germs.*"

"It does the same thing."

"No, it *doesn't.*"

He had to get out of there. He had to get out of the store, and out of the area. He wanted to just go and jump in some magic acid bath, something that would cleanse and purify his clothes and body, inside and out.

He grabbed the bottle of oral rinse and laid three dollars on the counter.

"One short, dude," the clerk said.

"It's only a three-ounce bot—" Neal closed his eyes and sighed. "Never mind." He gave the clerk another buck and twisted off the cap as he headed for the exit. For the next ten minutes, he stood next to his car, swishing, sloshing, and gargling the bottle's contents. It was no use. He couldn't wash the taste from his mouth. Or the stench from his upper lip.

He got into his Acura and sped off. He'd take the back roads, making sure he reached the Agency even faster than if he'd taken the highway. He sure as hell could maneuver a vehicle more smoothly and successfully than he could a woman's body. His experience with the Kat had certainly confirmed that.

She was in-call only, just as Neal preferred. And there was a fifteen-year age difference, also as he preferred (he was too embarrassed to be with anyone near his own age). A different ethnicity? Check. She wasn't anything close to Irish, not even a so-called Black Irish like himself. And he'd stuck to his aliases —"NumberJuan" on email and cell, and "Juan" in person. Everything was working, except for the one thing that never really worked.

He wasn't a virgin. He was something worse. *Inept.* He couldn't hold a girlfriend because he had no technique. Sloppy kisses and awkward caresses had yet to impress any. He did have what he once thought of as a secret weapon, over eight inches long. But it didn't take long for him to recognize that wasn't enough. *It's not the size that counts; it's what you do with it.* His sexual adulthood had been a progression from wet-noodle wielder to—with the assistance of a little yellow pill—cannon carrier, one that refused to fire when he was with a partner (though he did just fine on his own).

His lifelong dream of having a child was fading with each passing day. Thirty-five years out of his mother's womb and he still was no closer to being able to sow his own seed, not for the lack of trying. After thirty minutes of fumbling around with a woman, unable to even come close to ejaculating, his interest in satisfying her steeply declined. Frustration was a mood-killer no drug could reverse.

When his partners' reactions passed from "That's okay, baby" through yawning to "What the fuck . . . Are you gay?" he decided he needed practice. He bought a red smartphone and a new account to match; then he hit the backpages. He scheduled appointments with escorts who operated far from his neighborhood and his other regular haunts, but not *too* far. A Heartland Security agent using most of his personal time to make long-distance trips would quickly raise suspicion and potentially call down the wrath of superiors.

He'd been successfully elusive for six months now. But practice wasn't making perfect; it was just making him sick.

Fifty years old and heavyset, Lady Kat initially seemed promising. She'd agreed to meet him in her motel room on Saturday morning, 11:00, roughly two hours before he'd have to head in for his shift. Neal performed his usual surveillance ahead of time. As a member of the Agency's elite Peacemakers, a special-mission unit, he damn sure knew how to stay invisible while scouting territory, ensuring it was safe to enter. He'd perfected that skill, at least. Good thing the Heartland Security Agency was interested in hiring Peacemakers rather than Lovemakers.

Lady Kat was big, but voluptuous. A pleasing smile and gorgeous eyes that seemed to shift back and forth between green and blue both relaxed and aroused him. The body-rub he'd explicitly come for went well enough, even if her palms felt like she'd been laying brick with her bare hands. After she disrobed and they began entangling for what he'd implicitly come for, things went downhill—in more ways than one. He kissed her on the forehead and steadily made his way south. Her skin was sticky but tasty, as if she'd used maple syrup for lotion, but her thong, the one piece of clothing she'd kept on, smelled like the kitchen of a fast burger joint and had the greasy taste to match. He made sure the thong stayed on, and he stayed away from the patch for the rest of the hour.

He'd left the room with a mild feeling of nausea and something verging on a migraine, but the lingering odor in his nostrils and film on his tongue were what he most wanted to rid himself of before arriving at work. He could take a shower once he got there.

He couldn't help but appear as a heap of something one would wisely steer clear of if spotted in one's path. And most of his coworkers were wise. Unfortunately for his unit partner, she had no choice but to get close.

"You're almost late," Katrisha said.

"Almost." Neal dropped his bag in his chair and rummaged through his desk drawers.

"Why are you so shiny?" she asked.

He answered with a more important question. "Do you have any mouthwash?"

Katrisha sniffed. "Is that coconut oil?"

"Like *strong* mouthwash?" Neal repeated.

She shook her head. "Why didn't you get some on the way in?"

He smirked as he pulled his toothbrush out of the drawer. "Because I was almost late."

Katrisha shifted her eyes downward and nodded. "How'd you know? You're not wearing your watch."

Neal followed her eyes and dropped his brush. "Shit . . . Oh *shit*!"

The watch was Agency-issue, a prototype of a device developed in conjunction, and in *secret*, with a private contractor. As Neal understood it, the device was designed to connect with the nervous system and somehow enhance the body's electrical activity to the point where the air around the skin, the tiniest fraction of an inch, acted as a force field of some kind; they were experimenting with watches before they moved on to neural implants. Neal and other select Peacemakers were to wear the devices out in the field, testing them in action so they could be studied and improved. They looked like normal digital watches, almost exactly like Neal's old one, so he thought nothing of taking it off with the rest of his clothes and laying it on Lady Kat's nightstand. When it came time to leave, he was far more worried about getting the hell out of there without vomiting.

"Go back home and *get* it." Katrisha usually wasn't one to get emotional. She was professional through and through, believing wholeheartedly in the Agency's mission and following orders without question. What he saw in her eyes now was fiery intensity, so much of it her irises seemed to glow. Even though Neal was her senior in the unit, and her mentor, he'd screwed up, and she wasn't going to stand for it.

"It's not at home."

"Where is it?"

"It's . . . not at home." He wasn't sure what to say. Several years back, in the aftermath of President Sullivan cheating on his wife and being murdered for it, the law euphemistically dubbed the "Mistress Act" made prostitution and other pay-to-play sexual activities a severe crime, punishable by a minimum three-year prison sentence. One strike and you're in. To survive as an escort these days, one had to be smart and discreet: accept cash only, and for companionship only; the word "sex" and common terms for sexual activities were never to be mentioned in an escort's presence, not even in private settings. Not all those who advertised in the backpages knew the unspoken rules. Neal knew to only pick those who'd been advertising for some time; they were the ones who best knew how to stay out of jail and protect their clients. Now, he felt as naked as he'd actually been in Lady Kat's den.

"Neal, you need to get that watch back. If it—"

"Falls into the wrong hands—I know, I know." He waved her off as he hustled toward the stairs and pulled out his red smartphone. He wasn't about to risk a call. Even a text was too chancy within a building housing those dedicated to surveillance and security. He did send Kat a brief, cryptic email while making his way to the parking garage. He didn't expect a reply before he got back to the motel, but he wanted to try to give her a head's up he was coming.

He unlocked his Acura.

"We're taking the SUV."

"The fu—" Neal almost dropped his phone at the sound of Katrisha's voice. "Were you *following* me?"

"We're on Agency time now. Neither of us is off duty. Wherever you're going, I'm going."

Neal muttered three obscenities before following his partner to the black armored vehicle. Katrisha settled herself in the driver's seat as she asked, "So, we're not going to your place?"

"Just get us out of the garage," Neal said. "I'll guide you."

She drove the speed limit, but it still seemed a little too fast for him. Maybe because his brain had slowed down, inversely proportionate to the millions of rapid thoughts he'd had after seeing his bare wrist.

"What did you do this morning?"

Katrisha's question was a casual attempt at small talk, but in

his ears the words were the drip-drop beginning of an interrogation.

"I had brunch," he said after a moment.

"On Saturday?" she asked. "Who around here serves brunch
on Saturdays?"

"Someone who shouldn't."

The vehicle was silent until they crossed the city line, offi-
cially exiting Indianapolis. Katrisha sped up, edging over
the limit.

"Where?"

Neal sighed. "The Perfection Inn. About two miles down."

They parked in the guests' section. Neal unbuckled and held
up his hand as Katrisha opened her door.

"Would you mind letting me check this out alone?" he asked.

She furrowed her brow.

"Just stay here and call in," he said. "See where we're
supposed to go next."

She seemed content with this, softening her eyes as she
closed her door. Neal got out and ran, rounded a corner, then
banged on door 204. After a minute of silence, he banged again.
He dialed the Lady on his red smartphone. No answer. And still
no response to his earlier email.

To hell with this. He tried to hear through the windows and
peer through the drawn curtains. It was possible she was with her
next appointment, but Neal was beyond caring—and he didn't
have time to go to the motel manager with an explanation (even a
false one) and request a key. His reputation, job, and freedom
were on the line. Such a sudden realization could really push
a man.

He drew his Glock and fired at the window. He was built like a
running back, but he had no hope of breaking down a dead-
bolted door without injuring himself. The window was safer—
for him, if not for whomever was on the other side.

He kicked in most of the glass, brushed aside the curtains,

and crawled through. There was no trace of the Kat. No clothes, no toiletries, no odors . . . and no watch. The room was clean. The woman must've checked out right after Neal had left.

This time, before he could leave, his partner, someone who was probably the motel manager, and several onlookers gathered at the broken window and now-open door. Neal took a deep breath and calmly held up his HSA badge. The onlookers scattered. The manager backed away from the door. When Katrisha cleared her throat and flashed her badge, the manager glanced and scrambled away.

People, particularly people in the Midwest, knew why the HSA had been founded. Most folks harboring memories of immoral deeds shied away from the agents, lest they end up *disappeared*. Of course, that was just an urban legend among Middle Americans. If one cheated on his wife with a married woman, or had sex with a child, HSA agents wouldn't just drop out of the blue and throw the offender into a black hole. The offender would get a trial first.

Neal was getting the first taste of his trial now.

"What the hell is going on, Neal?" Katrisha stood in the doorway, glaring again with the fire in her eyes. This time, it was less a poetic impression; he actually thought her eyes flickered.

"Let's talk in the car." He walked toward it. "You called in to the Agency?"

Katrisha nodded.

"What'd they say?"

"Get back to the Agency."

They said nothing more until Katrisha had put several miles between them and the motel. She wasn't going to repeat her earlier question; she apparently felt she'd said enough. She was a good agent. She knew how and when to apply the silent treatment on one with a damaged conscience.

"I . . ." Neal cleared his throat. "I was with a woman this morning. I left the watch on the nightstand. An accident."

"Could be more serious than that," Katrisha said quietly, "depending on what she does with it."

Neal gazed through the windshield, looking at nothing.

"What type of woman was she?" Katrisha asked. "Young? In her twenties? What color were her nails? How was her hair styled?" She asked three questions in the amount of time it took Neal to answer one. She was the sharpest mentee he'd ever had. A description of the woman—everything from her appearance, age, and the way that she spoke—could help them narrow down the type of people with whom Lady Kat might run around, and the type of locales she might frequent. But when Neal gave Katrisha the Lady's age and appearance, the junior agent seemed stumped. Escorts of this type were rare; most either were or tried to pass themselves off as twenty- or thirty-something models.

"She probably operates alone," Katrisha said, "or with a single partner. A boyfriend, or a permissive husband."

Neal was shocked that Katrisha had remained so professional after his admission. Maybe she just wanted to do her duty for the day—retrieve the watch—before shepherding his termination and imprisonment.

"Whores like that . . ." Katrisha mused. "She's probably a swinger."

Neal's red phone buzzed. He'd received a text.

U want me? Ow!

It was Lady Kat. Neal texted back, responding with the obvious question. He received a less obvious answer.

Meat 2nite at SXS. 9:30.

"What are you doing?" Katrisha asked.

"SXS." He ignored her sharp tone. "You know what that is?"

"It's a swinger's club on—" She paused before shifting her tone again. "Is that that bitch? Hand me your phone!"

"Just keep driving," Neal said.

"Hand me your phone! I can trace—"

"Keep *both* hands on the wheel," Neal said. "She's already

switched phones. I only know it's her because she included some stupid puns in her messages. She'll switch again before you or I can do anything."

"She's at the SXS? Let's go."

"*No*. She said 9:30. She wouldn't have given us a location if she were there already." Lady Kat was going to be more trouble than he thought. Swinger, escort, whatever—she was starting a dangerous game. For the first time, Neal considered whether she probably—somehow—had targeted him, possibly just to get the watch.

"So we're just going back to headquarters to twiddle our thumbs till then?"

"We're going to get backup," Neal said, "and to strategize. I have the feeling she's not all we're going to have to deal with tonight."

Katrisha mumbled something.

"How did you know, just off the top of your head, SXS was a swinger's club?" he asked.

"It's my job to know. It's *our* job."

Neal stayed silent for the rest of the drive.

RUFUS, the head of Indiana's Peacemaker unit, appropriately and sufficiently chewed Neal out before allowing him to shower and change into his uniform.

The HSA had only one local branch in the state of Indiana. Ohio and Illinois both got two, while Michigan and Kentucky both had only one. Neal and his colleagues had spent countless hours discussing Washington's bias and debating whether Indiana could use one more office, say in Gary, or even in Evansville. But today he experienced a big benefit of working in a state's sole office: the top men more jealously guarded their own, happily ignoring protocol when it came to some of their best and more senior employees. Some of that had to do with a we-need-all-the-help-we-can-get mentality. But much of it had to do with turning a blind eye to stupid, minor crimes to focus on the perpetrators of bigger ones.

Neal was reprimanded but he'd keep his job, and take a slight reduction in pay—roughly the amount he'd probably spend on escorts over a six-month period. He considered that fair enough. The memory of his most recent wasn't going away any time soon.

Neither was the oil. He spent fifteen minutes in the shower to no benefit. Whatever it was, it certainly wasn't baby oil. He grumbled to himself as he dressed, mixing curses with vows to pick up stronger soap after work. He then hurried on to the planning room.

There were a dozen Peacemakers already waiting; that was half the number in the entire office. Katrisha, sitting up front, motioned for Neal to join her. Rufus then stood and explained the mission, gave some background about the club and its neighborhood, then asked Katrisha to take over. Before she could even stand and speak, she was hit with a question.

"Is it really going to require all of us?" one of the Peacemakers asked. "Can't three or four of us just go in undercover?"

"Two of us should go in undercover," Katrisha said, "me and Neal. Any more than that is too risky. But we'll need backup at every entrance and potential exit."

"For what?" another Peacemaker asked. "We're talking about perverts, here, not gangsters."

Katrisha and Rufus exchanged glances before the latter said, "You all know about the White Fire Virus. You've been briefed many times on what some of its carriers can do. You're damn right we're going into a den of sexual perverts, one or more of whom will likely be infected with the STD."

"Why else would this woman hole up there and send us an invitation?" Katrisha said.

Neal bowed his head. When he began his practice sessions

with escorts, he did consider STDs. He'd always worn a condom, but even a child knew rubbers didn't offer 100% protection. If Lady Kat had not just an STD but the strangest and most feared one of all . . .

What the hell had he done to earn this rotten spot?

"Neal will provide us with a description," Katrisha said. "I just want to say, don't trust your eyes. Anything that looks like . . . whatever—ghost, demon, or angel—*shoot* it. Multiple times. Washington won't let us quarantine these plague carriers, but . . . Well, use your best judgment, the judgment we've been trained to use."

Neal heaved his shoulders and sighed as the savvy agent retook her seat. It appeared the mentee was quickly surpassing the mentor on the levels of respect.

He stood and described everything about Lady Kat he could remember—how she looked, sounded, and smelled (eliciting chuckles), what she'd been wearing, and everything she'd told him during their moment by candlelight. He wasn't sure how this was helpful for the mission; part of him just wanted to confess as a way of absolving himself. Another part of him dwelled on the fact he was destined to live his life childless, having accomplished nothing meaningful outside of his low-paying job. Nothing beyond close friendships was in his future. And if he'd somehow contracted the Virus, a much worse fate would welcome him.

THE SXS WAS AS PACKED as expected for a Saturday night, and no one gave Neal or Katrisha any kind of hassle as they paid the cover and headed toward the bar. It helped immensely that Peacemaker uniforms were nothing like military or police uniforms. They came in a variety of colors and designs, were armored in the right places, stocked with hidden (and dangerous) goodies, and yet they were fashionable enough to wear among the urban public without raising suspicion. The style changed every so often to help prevent Peacemakers from being made. So far on this night, the uniforms were working like a charm.

The downstairs bar had about twenty stools; there were also a few booths and tables where folks could drink and chat; but the doors lining the walls were the main feature of the club. Once they became acquainted out in the open, couples, threesomes, foursomes, and whatever else were expected to go behind closed doors to fulfill their seductive promises. Ostensibly no money changed hands between partners, and no one was actually cheating, so whatever took place behind closed doors was perfectly legal. Neal guessed the second floor had at least twice the number of rooms.

He wasn't surprised such a place would draw such a large crowd. In today's society, it seemed more and more people were hooking up any way that they could and as often as they could, maybe—at least subconsciously—as some form of protest. Or maybe sex performed properly allowed its participants to achieve an ecstasy no drug could deliver. He could only speculate. Perhaps there wasn't much going on in their minds at all. Some of them may've simply viewed all potential partners as shiny packages under a Christmas tree, something to be obtained, unwrapped, and enjoyed for a few hours, then pushed aside under the couch or into the closet after boredom set in.

Such a thought couldn't help but creep into Neal's mind as they reached the bar. No sooner had they sat down when a man with an open shirt and hairy chest took the stool on Katrisha's other side.

"From the moment you walked through the door, I couldn't take my eyes off you." The gigolo managed to speak both loudly and clearly while somehow maintaining a toothy grin. "Want to tell me what makes you so beautiful?"

Katrisha faced him and seemed to say, "I have one billion parasites living in my skin and blood. They do all the hard work."

Neal wasn't sure what he'd heard, but he saw the gigolo's face contort into an anguished grimace as it seemed to reflect a greenish pale light. The man fell off his stool, landed on his arm, and then scrambled away, rubbing his arm while glancing over his shoulder, as if hoping Katrisha wasn't following him.

Neal shook his head. "What happened?"

Katrisha turned toward him and grinned. "Guess he got the wrong impression."

There was something in her eyes—a twinkle—as if tiny stars or gems were buried at the center of their globes. She shivered slightly then turned away, motioning for the bartender.

"What'll you have?"

"Information." Katrisha laid her badge on the bar and a hundred-dollar bill next to it. "Looking for Lady Kat."

The bartender eyed the bill, then Katrisha, then the bill again. He edged his fingers toward the money. Katrisha put her hand on top.

"We already know she's here. Fifty bucks is for you to tell us which room, and the other fifty is for telling us who she's with."

The bartender looked everywhere but at Katrisha, trying to figure who else was watching, or listening, before he leaned in. "She keeps a private room on the second floor. Number 42. She has a boyfriend. Acts as a bouncer in case her visitors get out of hand. He's here, but I don't know where."

"Just one guy?" Neal asked. "You sure?"

The bartender nodded.

"I'm sure," Katrisha said. "Their kind works in pairs." She released the hundred and said to the bartender, "More where that came from if you don't raise any alarms." He nodded again. She then turned to Neal. "I did my bit. You should probably lead from here."

Neal sighed and headed toward the staircase, ignoring every male, female, and whatever that smiled, winked, or tried to pull him aside. It wasn't hard to find room 42. It was almost directly opposite the stairs, and it had more space between it and its adjacent doors than most of the other rooms.

"I'll post by the door." Katrisha put her hand on one of her concealed weapons as she surveyed their surroundings, eyeballing potential hostiles, sizing them up, undoubtedly figuring which ones she could take out alone. It was what Neal normally would have done, but he was focused on the door. The hair on his arms and the back of his neck straightened. The day had turned increasingly complicated as it had progressed. Earlier, he was more than ready to storm Lady Kat's room, but now he felt he'd need protection—protection that Katrisha and the Peacemakers outside couldn't provide.

He knocked.

He barely heard the response over the noise behind him, but he swore it was a younger voice, sultrier than the one belonging to the woman he'd met that morning.

He entered.

His eyes immediately went to the St. Andrews cross and stayed there for a moment before moving on to the swings, the medical table, and the innumerable straps, canes, floggers, and other devices hanging from the wall. Under crimson lights, suffused with a New Age music that hadn't yet come of age, the room was a dungeon. His eyes drifted back to the cross.

"Did you come to play, or to pray?"

The Lady emerged from the shadows in the back of the long room, carrying a riding crop. Lady . . . or Mistress. Wearing a leather bustier and knee-length stiletto boots, the young woman seemed amused at his bewilderment.

His ears hadn't deceived him. This was not the woman he'd met with earlier. And, yet, it somehow was. She had the body and face of an athletic thirty-year-old. Her skin was darker, more dark chocolate than caramel. But those eyes . . . They glowed, unmistakably shifting between green and blue like malfunctioning traffic lights.

Neal swallowed. "I'm here for what's mine."

"Why don't you have a seat on the spanking bench, Number-Juan? I can give you everything you have coming." She approached, smiling and smacking the crop against her own bottom.

Neal's hand hovered near his concealed Glock.

"You're different," he said, "but I know you're you . . . Kat. I won't ask how, or why. Just give me the watch I left behind, and I'll leave you alone."

"Alone? Like you're destined to be?" She walked along the wall, fingering the various instruments and toys, reminiscing in a tone of false-fondness about their encounter that morning and all his inadequacies.

He'd been shirking lately, but he was still a seasoned agent. He knew what she was doing. He drew his gun. Before he could point it at her, Lady Kat grabbed two long, sharp, and pointy toys off the wall and came at him in a whirlwind.

She cut, sliced, slapped, and ducked—avoiding every offensive move, evading every defensive move—as she disarmed and rendered him naked in less than two minutes.

Neal was too thunderstruck to call for help, too shocked to retrieve one of his weapons, all of them now exposed at his feet. He only stood naked as he gazed at the grinning Lady.

"Still all slicked up, I see."

He glanced at his skin. His body glistened.

"What did you do to me?" he asked.

"I've begun to free you to be *you*." The Lady leapt at him, planting the stilettos under his chest and her hands around his neck before slipping him like a wet bar of soap and flipping him several feet backward. Neal braced himself for impact, but he never hit the floor.

The Lady had moved as if she were in a gyroscope, flipping and spinning around to catch him in a web of light cast by her fingertips. Neal's body splayed as if on the St. Andrew's cross, but he was in midair, gazing at the threads, each of them interwoven with black-and-crimson striped light and interspersed with glowing golden beads, all of it emanating from her skin and piercing his, simultaneously *stretching* and *tightening* his. He winced and grunted.

"Among its other benefits," Lady Kat said, "the oil will ensure this doesn't hurt nearly as much as it should."

"What . . . are you—" He sucked air through clenched teeth. The threads felt like tweezers digging into his skin for loose filaments and tugging when finding them.

"I'm just working out the kinks," she said. "Showing you the relationship between *pain* and pleasure. The grotesque and the *beautiful.* The *true* relationship between us—the deviants, the perverts, the sexually dysfunctional—and this world of false appearances."

It felt to Neal as if every inch of his body had sprouted its own tiny tongue and each was being forced to lick a 9v battery.

"We're not to be shamed, or mocked, or pitied," Lady Kat said. "We're to recognize our chosen status and band together to destroy the *One*. The One who put us in this state, making us constantly think there was something wrong with us, making us live a life of constant psychological and physical torment. We'll turn that torment into eternal ecstasy and *kill* our Creator. We start with ourselves, preparing for the session to end all sessions by freezing the body, then setting the soul on fire."

His peals of screams didn't begin to express what he felt. But they were enough to bring a rescuer. Katrisha rushed through the door, gun ready, and fired at the Lady. Neal had never known her to miss, especially at such a close range, but the shots may as well have been warnings. The Lady barely shifted a shoulder as the bullets plugged the walls.

"Ice!"

Neal assumed her cry was some kind of snarky dis to Katrisha, but he soon realized that the Lady was calling for her own backup. A coal-black man the size of a riding mower and wearing nothing but a thong came barreling from the back of the room. Katrisha aimed her gun, but the man embraced her before she could get off a shot. He held her in a bear hug and withstood her struggles and kicks without so much as a grunt as he carried her to the back of the room, which swallowed them both in shadows.

Kat's hands remained pointed at Neal, weaving the strings of light, vibrating them. He was no longer in pain. As she'd promised, it now felt pleasurable, as if he were receiving the best massage of his life.

The Lady lowered her arms. He remained levitating. Not only were his physical senses slightly enhanced, he was more in touch with his intuition. His sixth sense . . .

" . . . I have it, don't I?" he asked. "The Virus . . ."

"The Creator's last laugh at us," Lady Kat said. "Not content to just have our natural desires make us outsiders, the Fool wanted to punish us with what some call a disease. But, Ice and me, we call it a blessing. We *know* it's a blessing."

Ice. Neal remembered why he was here. He remembered Katrisha. He looked toward the back of the room and focused. His eyes converted the ebon shadows into white steam as his sight cut through the murk and he saw the big guy trying to strap the ball-gagged but still-struggling agent to a modified dentist's chair.

Neal unsteadily lowered himself to the floor. Once sure of his footing, he rushed toward them. He stopped when he felt hundreds of icicle-needles sticking his backside, increasing as rapidly in number as in cold-sharp intensity.

"Don't interfere," Kat said. "That betrayer is overdue for her punishment."

All the babble about killing some "One," blessings, and betrayals meant nothing to Neal. He was overwhelmed already by his own personal torture and revelation. And he didn't like what he saw happening with Katrisha. He didn't know or care what exactly was holding him back. He only focused on the big man, glaring at him with all the frustrated anger that had been pooling inside him. He neither blinked nor flinched when a gauzy red overshadowed his vision as his sight telescoped, focusing on the big man's ear.

Ice's head jerked back as if he'd been shot. He recovered and glared at Neal.

"Knotty!" he called. "Let him go! If he wants to try to melt me, let him come up and do it to my face!"

Neal turned around as best he could and saw that the Lady had both hands outstretched. Knotted, parti-colored strings of light that seemed to emanate from her fingertips were attached to his backside. She balled her hands into fists and lowered them, letting him go. Instead of rushing toward Ice as invited, Neal turned fully toward the woman.

"Whatever you are, whatever you're trying to do, to me or who-the-hell-ever, I don't care. But I'm not going to let you hurt my partner. Tell him to let her go."

"He already has."

Neal felt the steel-girder-like arms encircle his waist from behind. Ice didn't take his time as he had with Katrisha; he instead ran toward the back of the room, toward a black curtain, and leapt, making Neal take the brunt of the crash through the window and impact on the vacant parking lot two stories below.

The thick curtain minimized the pain and kept Neal mostly covered. But the wind had been knocked out of him. He was hardly in any shape to react as he saw Rufus and the other Peacemakers converging on the lot, weapons drawn. Ice was already on his feet, grinning. He seemed to be getting darker, blending into the night, in spite of the abundant light from the lot's several lampposts.

Neal's head was the only part of his body left uncovered. Lucky him. Lucky he hadn't cracked it open on the pavement. He wasn't ready to attempt to move his stinging arms and legs, but his eyes were mobile and strong—strong enough to throw a faint red, white, and blue tartan pattern over the entire landscape within his range of vision. As his sight focused ever closer on the square framing Ice, he shifted the lines, made them bolder, sharper, and imagined them carving the skin off of the big bruiser, making him easier to see in the nighttime, shaving off the coal-black, leaving what remained gleaming white.

Ice now appeared as a muscle-bound snowman in a thong, a grotesquerie who didn't stop grinning even after he noticed the change. He seemed to care nothing about the Peacemaker agents surrounding him, lining him up in their sights. He just looked at Neal.

"Man who had a force-field watch now has a skin-shearing stare. You're a natural." Ice pointed his thumb toward some of the agents. "They will love you—if they live through this."

Neal couldn't believe his eyes when he changed Ice's appearance—most of it was accomplished through a subconscious will to both expose and stop him—but what happened next was beyond both his belief and his control.

The man-mountain moved at the speed of an avalanche on fast-forward as he raced from Peacemaker agent to Peacemaker agent, choking them with one hand while smacking them across the face with another. He grinned all the while. The spectacle was perversely reminiscent of a game of freeze tag; as soon as Ice touched an agent, that agent froze in place. Ice managed to touch them all without any of them getting off a shot.

The big man stopped running but kept grinning as he loomed over Neal. His skin seemed embedded with miniscule ice-flakes, each of which glinted and glimmered in the light.

Crystals of some sort actually were embedded in his skin—a step up, Neal guessed, from mere piercings and tattoos. But the sparkles only momentarily held his attention. He was more drawn to something on Ice's arm, a relatively tiny gadget he hadn't noticed before due to there being so much else to notice about the big man.

Ice held up his left wrist. "This little watch of yours has done wonders to enhance my talents. On any other night, I would've just snapped their necks or something."

Neal tried to get to his feet, struggling with the curtain and his own disorientation as he realized the watch's properties may've somehow had a hand in helping protect him during his fall.

Ideally, even now, the prototypical watches were supposed to envelope the wearer in a skintight electromagnetic field that would act as an imperfect force field. Once the necessary adjustments were made after the testing phase, the perfect device would have the ability to warp space and time within the field, make the wearer more agile, give him or her the ability to turn invisible, and bestow many other benefits that could even the odds in a battle with evil—the evil primarily being outlaw Virus-carriers. Those who could, without the aid of any devices, manipulate types of electromagnetic radiation—mostly visible light, infrared radiation, and x-rays. But they were growing more powerful, particularly those Virus-carriers classified by the HSA as "The Infinite-Definite." They had honed their abilities to such a degree they were considered less than human and more like supernatural creatures. The terrorists had no leaders, but they operated in pairs, causing mayhem, spreading chaos. Pairs like Ice, and—

"Knotty!" Ice was looking up toward where he'd barreled through the window.

Still dizzy but on his feet, Neal hesitantly turned and looked up.

Lady Kat—*Knotty*—was hovering outside the window. She was holding a flogger in her left hand. A web the color of holly leaves and fruit emanated from her outstretched right hand to fill the space of the broken window. Katrisha's unconscious and naked body was stuck in the middle.

Neal knew it would be futile, but he shouted it anyway. "Let her go!"

Knotty smiled and descended as if riding an invisible elevator. She stopped roughly ten feet from the ground, maybe as far as she could go without losing control of the web. "What would you give for her?"

"Keep the damn watch!" Neal shouted.

"We don't care about your toys," Knotty said. "We have our own."

"Then why did you steal it?"

"I didn't. You left it behind, remember?"

She had him there.

"I was simply going to hold on to it as a keepsake," Knotty said. "But once Ice and I took a closer look at it . . ."

"What the hell do you want from me?" Neal asked.

Knotty gave him a smile that seemed equally seductive and malicious. "I've had my eye on you for a while, agent. You see, Katrisha here is . . . an old friend of mine. And I've been very interested in her attempts to uphold *morality* in light of what she'd been involved with in her past."

Neal knew nothing about it, and wasn't sure he wanted to. Though it was very clear that Katrisha, too, was a Virus-carrier.

"You want your toy back?" Knotty said. "Ice, give it to him."

Ice unfastened the watch from his wrist and tossed it at Neal. It landed somewhere in the folds of the curtain.

"I want Katrisha back," Neal said. "And I want all the other agents released from whatever this thing did to them."

"You may have all that," Knotty said, "in exchange for your help."

"*What*?"

"I long ago sensed you had a latent form of the Virus. And I used a little bit of, shall we say, *sensual* magick to help bring out the best in the worst. Thank my own *black-fantastic* arts, agent. Most people discover they have the Virus when it puts their body through *hell*—seizures, vomiting, mind turned inside out . . . and that's the least of it. You should be licking my stilettos. I made your transition *smooth*."

"Why?" Neal asked. "Why did you do this?"

"During one of our recent . . . *play* sessions, Ice and I happened upon a dirty little secret. *Your* dirty little secret."

Neal shook his head. "My—?"

"Your Agency has a secret unit composed entirely of magick-enhanced Virus-carriers. The chief one—*Violet Valentinus*—has been working on building a prison camp located in another dimension. Your agency thinks he's fully in their employ, but Valentinus believes himself to be an *angel*, an agent of the same Creator who is punishing us, the same Fool who is having a laugh at us. In the service of this Fool, Valentinus has been attacking other Virus-carriers at random. Destroying their bodies and sending their souls to this prison for who knows what reason. Now that you've been turned out, he'll come after you, and probably soon. He's coming after all of us. Unless we stop him."

"I know you," Neal said. "I know your *kind*. You're *ID*. Infinite-Definite terrorists. Why should I believe or trust you?"

"Trust *this*," Ice said. "He's coming here. Tonight."

"Yes," Knotty said. "I've prepared a dark tantric trick that'll ensure he shows. Ice and I have a plan to stop him. With your help, it'll work."

"Why do you need help?" Neal asked with a sneer. "You two are so bad-ass. Why not take him on by yourselves?"

"Valentinus is used to encountering our *kind*, as you put it, in pairs," Knotty said. "Based on our own research, we figure three is his unlucky number."

"Three is a magick number, after all," Ice said.

"Then why did you need me?" Neal asked; then, though he almost hated to say it out loud, "Why not just use Katrisha?"

"We are," Ice said with a chuckle. "As bait. We'll be doing a little ice-fishin' tonight."

"But you," Knotty said to Neal, "you're the type of guy Valentinus goes for. A true sexual misfit. He loves taking *our kind* down."

"We're going to hit him before he hits us," Ice said.

"You help us," Knotty said. "Ice will let your fellow agents go. Unfrozen. *Alive*."

"And what'll you two do then?" Neal asked.

"We'll go on our merry way."

"And Katrisha?"

"That's the best part," Knotty said. "She'll be my special gift to you . . ." There was that mixed-signals smile again. "I remember all you told me during our sweet, *sweet* time together this morning."

Neal briefly averted his gaze. He was well past the point of blushing, but her words still hit a soft spot.

"You help us," Knotty said, "you get her—in whatever condition you want her. Obedient. Totally compliant. All yours, mind and body. Willing to serve all your imaginable desires . . ."

Neal could no longer stand to look at the twisted expressions on Knotty's face. He turned his attention to Ice but saw the same damn thing. They and their words were beyond distasteful—but . . .

He wondered if Rufus and the others, despite their frozen state, could see and hear what was happening. None of them had moved an inch since Ice had tagged them. And, Katrisha . . . Was she conscious, or was she taking all of this in? What were all of them thinking of Neal? He was their only potential knight—a knight in no armor. He was the reason they were here in the first place. He was the reason the whole force had been taken out by a couple of deviants. He, another deviant.

HSA briefings on Infinite-Definite associates had always portrayed them as light-manipulating zombies, diseased and mostly mindless terrorists, bent on spreading chaos and confusion until the world exploded. These two certainly weren't mindless. But were they crazy? He didn't know anything of the secret agent they mentioned—this *Violet Valentinus*. But they seemed hell-bent on conjuring and killing him. And if he helped them . . . Well, even if Katrisha weren't unconscious, he could always attempt to make the case he was being coerced. After all, he was. He was bargaining for the life of his fellow agents. He had no other out—for, undoubtedly, if he refused to help them, he'd be killed, as would every other agent on site.

"Choose now, agent," Knotty said. "Our window is growing smaller."

Their window. Neal gazed at Katrisha's nude, splayed body as he thought of Knotty's promise. Promises could be broken, and refused, but . . .

"Okay," he said with a sigh. "What do you need me to do?"

"We made some adjustments to your gadget," Ice said. "Put it on."

Neal had no choice but to drop the curtain and totally reveal his nakedness as he went through the folds to retrieve the watch. After he found and fastened it, his hand's skin color immediately changed. One finger black with ice-white nail, another finger white with coal-black nail, a white-and-black checkered pattern across his hand, up his arm . . . "The fu—" He gaped while his skin color changed in a pattern that seemed both haphazard and meticulously planned until he was totally black and white.

"A safeguard," Knotty said. "An offense as well as armor against the one who is coming. Ice and I have our own. Now, get ready."

He was a naked chessboard, one upon which no queen would ever tread. At this point, he wasn't sure what "ready" meant.

"Watch for any fluctuations in the air," Knotty said. "When he appears, look at him—*hard*—let your new sense take over. Ice and I will do the rest."

Neal noticed Ice's skin color had not changed back to black. His new abilities were a mystery to him. He knew vaguely he could manipulate light—but changing someone's skin pigment? Embedded crystals or no embedded crystals, had Neal actually done that to Ice, or had that just been Ice's reaction to something else Neal was intuitively trying to do? Hell, would intuition be enough against this Valentinus?

Knotty had ascended back up to the second floor. She was eye-level with Katrisha and speaking something that sounded like melodic gibberish. A lot of random, rhyming words. Watching and listening, Neal realized for the first time the knotty similarity between the names Lady *Kat* and *Kat*risha. How coincidental was that?

The web vibrated and glowed even brighter as Knotty moved closer to her captive. Katrisha's body trembled, appearing to experience the same frisson Neal accomplished after a successful session of auto-eroticism. Knotty brought her face closer to hers, her lips closer to hers.

"What is she doing?" Neal asked.

"It's just magick," Ice said. "Nothing you need to worry about."

Knotty finally stopped speaking in tongues and kissed the woman, using lips and tongue while keeping her eyes wide open. The web vibrated even more violently as visible waves of violet electricity seemed to emanate along the strands, outward from the center.

Neal didn't want to look away, but he sensed something happening somewhere above him. He titled his head upward and saw a patch of shimmering air high up in the sky. The shimmer became an electric-blue tear, and through it flew a large, screeching eagle seemingly composed entirely of violet light.

The frozen Peacemaker agents collapsed as Ice ran to a far corner of the lot. Neal figured he'd had to concentrate at least a little to keep them in place, but now that the big game was here, Ice had to shift all of his focus, letting his previous victims sleep. At least Neal hoped they were sleeping.

The screeching eagle dove straight for Knotty. The woman certainly was a professional . . . *something*. She maintained the web as she whipped her flogger toward the eagle, forcing it to rapidly molt most of the feathers of light from its body. They fell like fiery confetti but burned out quickly. The wings on its back were unaffected but the thing slowed as its body resolved itself into a man's—a giant, nude man with a head shaped like some kind of wolf.

Valentinus.

Now at a closer range than his initial appearance, his body appeared at least eight feet in length, but the wings of violet fire spanned at least twice as wide.

Valentinus had slowed his progression toward Knotty but didn't stop as he closed the distance—roughly forty feet, thirty feet, fifteen feet—until Knotty suddenly stopped flogging with her left hand and swung her right.

The entire web, Katrisha included, flung toward the winged thing. Valentinus was unable to swerve or stop as Katrisha's body involuntarily embraced him and the web of honey-colored light enwrapped around them both.

Valentinus's wings snuffed out, but the embracing two hung in the air long enough for Ice—who'd begun running when the web was tossed—to make an astounding leap at the two and rapidly slap his hands on several parts of both bodies before dropping again.

Katrisha and Valentinus slowed in their descent, until Ice made another run-and-touch, and then another. The big man moved like an Olympic sprinter, or maybe more like an Olympic skier, one used to taking to the air and flipping, maneuvering with ease. When Ice was done, the embracing two descended no more. They hung as if in suspended animation inside a transparent cocoon.

"Now, agent!" Knotty yelled. "Gaze at them! Think! Concentrate! *Glaze* them!"

Neal gazed at the target, but he wasn't sure what to think. Katrisha had her arms wrapped around a giant man who had the head of a wolf. Both were naked. Both were seemingly asleep. It was like something out of an exceedingly perverse fairy tale.

"Stare in *anger*," Knotty said. "Remember what I told you he *is*. Remember what *you* told *me* this morning.

Neal continued to stare, and started to remember. He'd told Knotty about the lack of intimacy in his life, and his desire to have a child. And now he was looking at . . .

Knotty. She'd set up this pose. On purpose. To humiliate him. To *trick* him. Knotty and Ice had set him up to take out not only their enemy but his own partner as well. As if he hadn't already dug himself into enough trouble today.

Knotty met his eyes. She seemed to know what he was thinking. She turned toward the open window, preparing—Neal assumed—to whisk herself back into her playpen for cover.

He wasn't as stupid as he looked.

He focused on her head and thought of fireworks, bursting in a splendid array of colors. He soon heard the screams that often accompanied such a display, but they were all coming from Knotty, whose hair was popping and crackling and blazing like wiry sparklers.

She fell backward in an arc toward the ground. Ice raced to her rescue. Neal focused on his skin and played connect the dots with the embedded crystals, those crystals that twinkled like stars.

Ice hollered and fell on his face, shrieking, as fires the size of match heads flared up all over his body. He rolled on the ground until—small miracle—Knotty crash landed on top of him.

Both appeared to be unconscious. Neither was burning anymore—most likely because Neal stopped focusing on either one. His attention drifted upward.

Valentinus was awake and ensured that any who might be looking believed it by flaring his violet eagle's wings at a span that seemed a mile long. He descended, cradling Katrisha's body in his arms as he landed just a few feet in front of Neal.

Neal didn't move. He may've been in awe. He may've been scared. Or he may've just been too exhausted. He wasn't entirely sure, but he stood his ground as Valentinus approached.

Neal gazed as the wolf's head shapeshifted into a man's. His body had an odd skin tone. Vanilla glazed with violet. As Valentinus neared, more and more visible light—*cold fire*—gathered about that strangely hued body, waves of violet, indigo, and blue that shrouded most of him like a philosopher's robe. The wings still flared behind him, but they'd been greatly reduced in size. Neal wondered why he wasn't blinded by the whole spectacle as he gazed at it. He guessed it was an effect of his new condition.

Valentinus stopped a few paces in front of him. Neal looked up into those deep purple eyes. The angel really was about eight feet tall.

"Take her." The angel appropriately spoke with a voice that, in Neal's ears at least, pealed like thunder.

Neal allowed him to lay Katrisha's body in his arms. He looked down into her face. She did not appear to be breathing.

Valentinus stepped backward and leaped several dozen feet into the air, flipped, and landed next to Knotty and Ice. He picked the latter up by his throat, lifted him off the ground, and said something Neal couldn't understand.

Ice regained consciousness and began to struggle. Valentinus thrust his free hand into Ice's chest, as if he really were made of snow, and ripped out a bloody lump that could've only been his heart. The blood glistened as streams of light flowed from Valentinus's eyes and mouth into Ice's. The latter's body disintegrated as if it had been reduced to shaved ice.

Perhaps it really had. The mass on the ground seemed to melt away as Knotty stirred.

More alert than she initially appeared, Knotty lunged at

Valentinus the moment she saw him. He grabbed her by the throat and gave her the same treatment as her partner. Her skin darkened and sunk in on itself until he let her go. She disintegrated into a pile of ashes.

Valentinus met Neal's eyes. This time, the agent was ready to run away, but having Katrisha in his arms would've made it difficult. It wouldn't have mattered anyway. The angel closed the distance between them in a blink. He loomed over Neal, staring down into his eyes.

"Guess it's my turn now," Neal said with a sigh.

"It would have been," Valentinus thundered, "if you had actually allowed yourself to be tricked by them."

Relief delivered in a way that was not at all comforting. Neal shouldn't have expected anything less at this point. "They said *this*—the pattern of my skin, my watch—it would all protect me from you."

"And you believed them," Valentinus said. "I suppose they did not have IQ tests for Heartland Security agents when you joined."

And there was the insult he was expecting.

"They were simply mocking you," Valentinus said. "And me. Your abilities have been slightly enhanced due to that piece of technology, but you would have not been able to stop me."

"Stop you from taking me to some kind of extra-dimensional prison," Neal said. "A lockup for sexual *weirds*. Did they lie about that, too?"

Valentinus didn't answer right away. His eyes flashed as he broke eye contact with Neal, looking him up and down, before responding. "Their souls are now in an extra-dimensional realm under my supervision. They will not be able to escape or harm anyone ever again. The two mockers, they turned your skin into a mockery of a prisoner's uniform from years past. They had no intention that you would be saved. You were to suffer the same fate as them, or go in their place."

"Why?"

"They were dangerous thrill seekers, like all the other two-person cells of The Infinite Definite. *Errorists*. These two, unlike many others, were proficient in various forms of dirty but powerful magick. I came after them several days ago, and failed. Since then, their Modus Operandi has been to seduce the naïve into going along with their plans to destroy me. Each time, after drawing me out and attacking, and realizing their latest plan will not work, they fled, leaving the seduced to face my wrath. This was their third attempt, and their last."

"Katrisha . . ." Neal looked at the woman in his arms. "The other agents . . . Are they dead? They've been out for a while. Katrisha isn't breathing."

"They are in an altered state. Neither dead nor alive at the moment. But I will take care of them."

The angel's last sentence was a little too cryptic for Neal. He practically blurted, "Are you really on our side?" he asked. "The HSA, I mean. Are you one of our agents?"

"I am an agent of One yet to be born. One who will set right all that seems imperfect in this world, all that is odd in the sight of its inhabitants."

Still a bit too cryptic for Neal, but what else should he expect from an angel? "What now?" he asked, hoping for something a little more straightforward.

The angel's eyes blazed before he said, "I can let you live the rest of your days on this Earth as you are now, or I can offer you a release."

If those were his two choices, the answer was obvious, but "What do you mean by 'release'?" Neal had been with enough escorts to fear the answer.

"I can send your soul to where the Errorists have gone," Valentinus said.

Neal had a clear response to that.

"Or," Valentinus said, "I can give a new role. A redeeming role."

The crypticism had crept back—but, really, what were his other options?

"Make the same offer to Katrisha," Neal said. "After everything that's happened tonight, I doubt she can go back to the Agency. I doubt she wants to. But what do I know? She deserves to make an informed decision."

"And your decision?"

Neal sighed. "The new role, I guess."

"Lay the woman down, gently."

Neal turned to his left, walked a few paces, and did as instructed. Straightening, he again made eye contact with the angel.

"Every creature living today was born imperfect," Valentinus said as he moved a step closer, "with a defect. Some poets might call it a necessary flaw in the constitution of a creature. And it is necessary, once recognized, for one to embrace and overcome it on the way to perfection. Sacrifice the chunk of ice in oneself to become a being suffused with the passion of eternal fire."

Valentinus thrust his right hand into Neal's chest. Neal didn't have a chance to flinch, let alone move as the fingers clutched his heart and his body shuddered with an ice-cold frisson.

Valentinus retracted his hand as quickly as he'd thrust it forward. The last thing Neal saw was the angel holding up a fiery lump in front of his face, which had melted into a skull with eyes and mouth filled with violet flames.

NEAL STOOD IN A WIDE, seven-walled room made entirely of glass, or something that approximated glass. The walls and ceiling gave view to a fathomless green-bluish haze populated with black phantomlike streaks. The room somehow existed simultaneously on Earth and outside of the known universe. It was a meeting room. A planning room.

To Neal's right was a man who could create and remotely control holographic facsimiles of himself. To Neal's left was a woman whose every word came out as a flying insect of light, each one ready to sting or bite. And behind him were three others with varying abilities that had some connection to light and sound.

And Neal—he was the one who could, among other magick tricks, generate limited-range force fields and cast expertly woven nets of light with his eyes or fingers, nets that could freeze, burn, and do other cruel things to evildoers.

He and the rest were all listening to a briefing by the Equinox, a more-than-ten-foot-tall man-creature who had talons for hands, cloven hooves for feet, and a unicorn's head. Heaven knows what all he could do; Neal had only been told that he could transmute matter into energy.

The Equinox was a "consultant"—from where exactly Neal wasn't privy to know. The rest of the room's occupants served in the black ops group known as the Dark Artzmen, or those who wore—quite literally—parts of their own souls as skin. The whole operation was the pet project of an HSA official in Washington, a wise man with *magickal* connections. A man who believed the real-deal Apocalypse was coming and was doing everything he could to stop it. In light of everything that was transpiring on the Earth these days, the Artzmen group was quite a creative idea.

Katrisha had opted to stay with the Agency's branch in Indiana. She would no doubt be viewed very differently now that they knew she had the Virus, but she was in no danger of losing her job. In fact, Neal wouldn't be surprised if they promoted her. After all, the Agency needed all the help it could get.

The Equinox was briefing him and the others on a mission they were to undertake immediately. Gargantuan creatures were appearing in the far reaches of the globe. Some of them seemed to materialize out of thin air, others seemed to crawl out of the oceans. The Artzmen had to take them down as quickly and efficiently as possible.

Outside the walls, out in what Neal called the "ether," something that appeared like violet ball lighting bounced and streaked, raggedly zigzagged from one spot to another before blinking out altogether. *Valentinus*—off on another mission. Though he was the chief Artzman, he often worked independently on projects secret even to the rest of them. Whatever he did, he did it quickly. Rumors abounded that he operated in multiple places at once.

Neal owed him a lot. Valentinus had given his physiology a little extra tweaking, which served to enhance his innate abilities even more. So long as he stuck to the regimen required by the Artzmen, he would go far. Valentinus had also given him some words of wisdom: "Love is not about sex. Or friendship. Or companionship. It goes deeper. It's about *Creation*."

Neal had a purpose, and a place. He was no angel, not even a saint. He was more like a fighting monk, celibate and separated from humankind but dedicated to a singular, creative idea.

Finally, a suitable position.

ROGUE BEAUTY

I t's easy to kill ugly things.

The urge wells up like sexual desire, easing through the body, imbuing the soul as it pushes back against the disgusting assault on the senses. Only the repressed, the *normals* —the plain Janes and Johns—successfully suppress what their bodies are telling them to do. Yes, there are lines—but to the wise, those lines are blurry.

Only a despicable character would pass by a well-maintained flower garden and have a sudden urge to trample everything in sight. But consider a pretty girl of stable disposition passing by the front yard of a careless homeowner, one who has let weeds overtake the grounds to such an extent it appears to be a tallgrass prairie. Since the environment is clearly a reflection of the one charged with maintaining it, it would be easy to understand and excuse her taking a scythe to both owner and his property.

Only the most twisted among us would ever consider decapitating a puppy or putting a kitten in a blender. But if a sympathetic gal observed a wheelchair-confined boy with a stumped appendage and at least one other physical deformity, a boy prone to incessant drooling and spontaneous fits and violent outbursts, verbal and otherwise, she'd rightfully wonder how his parents could be so inhumane as to allow him to suffer incessantly and how society could allow the parents to let the boy live a life of unending misery and, while she wondered, her subconscious would nudge her into the role of merciful angel, a role the plain Janes and Johns would misinterpret as villainous.

Then there were the more complicated scenarios, those involving truly vile creatures, all aided and abetted by the Janes and Johns. This is where the lines surpassed blurry and twisted into wavering spirals. There were dimensions to true justice, shades to beauty...

My sunrise exercise could give me quite a charge.

I ran through a rumination of colorful scenarios and contrasts every morning while applying my makeup, and the runner's high sometimes became so overwhelming I inadvertently squeezed a steel canister out of shape.

My makeup came in reinforced containers, specially made. The powders and paints themselves had been specially formulated, concocted by doctors and scientists who'd devoted their careers to studying the White Fire Virus and devising ways to keep its carriers comfortable. The hope, perhaps, was that if the carriers felt comfortable enough, moral enough, *pretty* enough, they'd be more inclined to do whatever they could to tamp down their strange urges and not display the supernatural abilities that neither they nor the doctors nor the scientists truly understood. The same pharmaceutical company that sold the makeup also produced the prescription-only lotion I applied to my hands and forearms, my ankles and calves, and—on the days I was so inclined to wear an outfit that would leave it exposed to light—my midriff.

My authorized prescriptions had run out some time ago. But I had good connections. One of them stood in the bathroom's doorway, watching me, waiting for the day's agenda.

"Yesterday: whore chic," Bruce said. "Today: businesswoman bleak?"

"Necessary," I said as I applied eyeliner. "I need to charm my way through an office building, not a Marriott. Today's target is an old colleague."

"Yeah? From which profession?"

Touché. "The legal one."

Bruce guffawed. "The *really* shady one."

He looked ready to make a joke about the connection between prostitutes and lawyers, but I gave him the look that let him know I wasn't in the mood.

He shrugged. "Anyway, so long as you keep to your medications, it doesn't matter how you dress."

"Of course it does." I picked up the pencil and worked on my brows. "It takes a lot of energy to shift. And a lot of concentration to maintain. How I dress can hurt or help the whole operation."

"You want me to wait till you're finished?"

"I'm almost done here," I said. "Go get the black leather briefcase ready."

"Contents?"

"Persona: Jacquelyne Mae. Operation: Interview. Location: Law firm."

Bruce backed out of the doorway and headed toward the den.

I finished my makeup, went into my bedroom, and examined the complete package in the full-length mirror. A custom black dress stopping at the knees, cord belt, and citrine stud earrings. Appropriate for late September. Appropriate for an interview at a law firm. It was a pretty outfit. It would be even prettier when I added the matching jacket and handbag. And my face, when I remade it, would make the entire package absolutely *beautiful.*

But I wasn't quite there yet. Choosing shoes was always difficult. Beauty versus practicality: the former sometimes provided a decisive advantage when confronting certain enemies. Heels would be expected, and they would certainly complement my dress, but at some point I was going to need to break, run, and take some long jumps. Even though I could damn sure move quickly in heels, I couldn't sprint more than fifty meters in them without bruising myself. In some situations, they'd make for nice weapons. For today's job, flats would be more effective once shit hit the fan, but I certainly couldn't wear those to an interview.

Decisions, decisions—pretty, pretty decisions...

I chose black and gold-studded wedge sandals.

"Your briefcase, Miss Mae." Bruce poorly affected the tone of an English butler as he walked into the bedroom and laid the case on the bed next to the handbag. "The papers are inside." He held up his left hand. "Here's the wallet for your purse. Fake license, credit and debit cards, and one hundred and twenty dollars in cash."

"Lay it next to the handbag."

"Will you be needing any accessories?" Bruce asked.

"The thumb drives we discussed last night should be in the briefcase. Just the usual makeup and touch-up perfume in the handbag."

"Already done," Bruce said. "I meant anything sharp and shiny?"

"I'm going in soft," I said. "I *will* have to pass through a metal detector."

"So we're definitely not hitting a pimp this time?"

"A white-collar pimp," I said. "The worst kind."

"Which one from my list?"

"He wasn't on it. His name's Prakul Varman."

Bruce shook his head. "Not a familiar name to me. But you're going into this place to get him... You don't want to wait for him to come outside? Hit him on his way to lunch or coffee?"

"He doesn't get his own coffee. He has one of his girls do it for him—ditzy paralegals and chirping secretaries. Besides, we need to make a *statement*. I need to do it in his office so all his colleagues can see."

"You could just as well do it in his home. Film it, stream it over the internet while you run a blade across his—"

"*Bruce*, this firm is an important link in the chain. I need to get info I can only get from inside. Once we have it—"

"All right, Betty." Bruce nodded. "Got it."

"Besides, seeing the body freshly bled in front of them will be much different than his colleagues seeing it on a screen. Jaded souls, I'm sure they are."

"Yeah." Bruce chuckled. "Jaded souls we *all* are."

"While I'm inside, I'm going to need you to rendezvous with one of the suppliers. Pick up some more of my medications."

"For the skin?" Bruce asked. "Or for what's under?"

"Everything," I said. "I don't ever want to be in short supply of anything. Make your connection then get the car ready. And double check the traffic reports. My interview's at ten. I want to be at least fifteen minutes early."

Bruce left the room.

I opened the briefcase. Thirteen copies of Jacquelyne Mae's resume, five copies of each letter of professional recommendation, three blue pens, two black pens, and one red pen, a notepad, and two thumb drives. Plenty of room to spare for a blade or two, even the kind that wouldn't be picked up by metal detectors or a visual search—but no. Today I was resolved to rely solely on my prettier talents.

I'D SPENT much of the night studying the floor plans and the layout of the neighborhood. I'd obtained the most recent maps the day before. The firm had undergone some internal construction but the layout was pretty much the same as the last time I was there. I went over everything one last time in the car, ensuring I had all possible escape routes memorized.

Bruce said nothing during the drive. He knew I needed to

think. I broke the silence when we were about two blocks away from the target.

"Make a right here."

He did as instructed.

"Turn left up ahead then let the car idle," I said, "and keep an eye out."

It was time to complete the look.

I pulled down the visor and looked in the vanity mirror. As I silently recited a chant, my eyes drew in light, sipped it like liquid through a straw, stripped it down to filaments of radiation, and then spun the filaments out like living, coiling, intangible threads under my sole control. The ability to manipulate light was a Virus-carrier's curse or blessing, depending on how the carrier chose to live her life. I put the multitude of "living" light-threads to work on my face—tightening a spot here, re-coloring a spot there, erasing a scar, adding a well-placed freckle or two, making this area more prominent, making that area less so—until I really looked like a *Jacquelyne Mae*. A *beautiful* woman.

My viral condition and the skill I'd acquired to cope with it enabled me to change the appearance of my face and body with relative ease, and the special makeup allowed me to hold the look for a longer amount of time with a minimal amount of concentra-tion. The susceptible would believe I was the person I wanted them to think I was. The fools in the lawless firm would not only believe the illusion but *love* it.

Bruce whistled as his eyes took in the new me, then he shook his head. "Still seems like a lot of unnecessary trouble, Betty. You could easily turn yourself invisible, sneak in, do the deed, and walk out as, uh, pretty as you please."

I sighed as I pushed up the visor. Poor Bruce was still rela-tively new to this life. I'd tried my best when training him to be my faithful assistant. He occasionally did offer helpful advice, but oftentimes he just didn't get it. Such was a perk of not being a Virus-carrier.

"Invisibility," I said. "Camouflage. These take greater amounts of concentration and will. They're energy drainers. Once in, I'm going to need to focus on studying the layout. These floor plans were helpful, but this is still slightly unfamiliar territory. And even though I worked here in the past, I can't totally rely on what I once thought to be true."

"The supplier I'm meeting with is Montross," Bruce said. "You know his background. Should I let him in on what's up? His boys could provide backup."

I closed my eyes and sighed again. He still didn't have complete confidence in me. It was kind of sweet in a way, him wanting to ensure I remained safe, especially considering how we first met.

"I know what I'm doing, Bruce. I was trained by... Well, I was trained by some who have more abilities and skills than they have any honest right to have. I'll be better off without meddling."

He nodded. I got out of the car and circled around to his window.

"One day you may get to see me in action," I said, "from start to finish. Then you'll understand how getting in is the hard part. Easing out is relatively sublime."

As expected, lobby security was a breeze. Upon reaching fifty-plus employees, most firms and companies in Richmond went through the trouble of hiring security guards and installing metal detectors. Once a business reached fifty employees, ugly elements started to pay attention; if it wasn't ripe for robbing, it might be ripe for exploding. The terrorists, gangs, and cults proliferating the area were always in contention for the biggest score in dollars or body count.

Miss Pruden from Human Resources met me in the lobby's elevator bank. "Miss Jacquelyne Mae?" We shook hands. "So pleased to meet you." She pushed the "up" button. "How has your day been so far?"

"Progressing beautifully," I said.

We stepped inside the elevator. I scanned all four walls then cast my eyes upward. One obvious camera in the back right corner. I shifted my vision across the electromagnetic spectrum as I scanned the roof. Opening the service hatch would be a piece of cake, but I put it on the list of last resorts. I wasn't about to go scrambling around in an elevator shaft again. Not if I could help it.

"I hope you don't mind me saying how impressive your resume is, Miss Mae."

"Why would I mind?" I asked.

She shrugged. "Well, you're no stranger to law firms. You know that a copy of an interviewee's resume has been given to everyone she's likely to come into contact with."

I nodded. "True."

"But no one's supposed to comment on it except the people with whom you've scheduled interviews."

I smiled and nodded again. "I know how the process works."

"But I just wanted to say how grateful I am for the *pro bono* work you've done on behalf of abused and, uh, *sick* women. Those living in the House of Thomas shelters. People like you are an inspiration."

I lost my smile and swallowed. Residents of the HOT shelters were those with incurable diseases. Generally, only Virus-carriers, those afflicted with other extreme ailments, and liberal do-gooders were sympathetic to the work the shelters performed. My research hadn't led me to conclude anyone employed by this firm would do anyone any good; the item was only on the resume as some volunteer work Jacquelyne Mae had done fresh out of law school, a time when people were expected to do stuff just because it looked good on a resume, not because they actually believed in what they were doing. Was Pruden a Virus-carrier, one adept at hiding her condition, or a bleeding heart who'd slipped through the cracks? If she or anyone else here were a Virus-carrier, a trained one, I'd have to alter my strategy. I looked at her face, looked beneath the skin—x-rayed, magnified, and tried a few other optical tricks as well as I could without seeming blatantly odd. I didn't detect any parasites. She wasn't a carrier, just a bleeding heart. If she crossed my path on my way out, I'd try not to hurt her too badly.

"I try to do my best," I said.

We stopped on the tenth floor.

"You'll be meeting with Miss Shaw first," Pruden said as she led the way past the reception and through the hall. "Then one of the senior associates."

"Any partners?" I asked.

"Well, it's a little unusual for a first round. But, since you have such awesome credentials, maybe Miss Shaw can set something up, depending on schedules. Is there anyone in particular you'd like to try to see?"

"I have one or two in mind." I wasn't about to give anything away and risk losing the element of surprise. "I'll discuss with Miss Shaw."

Surreal artwork covered the walls, all by artists who'd tried hard to one-up or two-up Van Gogh. *Spectacular.* They were vibrant enough for me to use to my advantage if I needed any extra help escaping.

None of the offices I passed had doors, and half were empty. No surprise. The recession had been tough on almost everyone, including this once-mighty firm that in my day had filled all thirteen of its floors. But they weren't hurting that badly. Varman and his department were full of black-rainmakers. They were still bringing in the dollars just fine.

Shaw was a frumpy but seemingly affable woman in her mid to late 40s. I was expecting someone taller, leggier, more *angular*, and wearing just the right skirt and blouse to show off all the goods. Firms of this type usually put women of that sort in the HR and recruitment departments, putting up a good front to attract the right sort of hires. In fact, I would have been willing to bet women of that kind *were* to be found aplenty among this firm's recruiters, but they probably only met with the male prospects.

We exchanged introductions and shook hands. When invited, I sat in the chair in front of her desk and handed her a copy of my resume. Of course, she'd already read it, but she scanned it again, either to refresh her memory or to be polite. Before she could ask her first question, I reached back into my case and said, "Each of my references typed out a brief letter of recommendation. The letters include contact information for follow-up discussions." I handed her one copy of all five, all originally signed, though not by the people whose names were at the top. Bruce wasn't quite a master forger, but he was good enough.

"Impressive," Shaw said. "Most people just provide names, titles, and phone numbers for their references."

"I wanted to go the extra mile."

Shaw skimmed the letters and I skimmed my surroundings.

"So," she said, "you want to be an associate with our firm." She looked me up and down, taking in the entire package before her. "You know the recession has been hard on everyone, especially lawyers..."

Yeah—bullshit time. She asked her questions and I gave her the answers she wanted to hear, justifying my existence and intentions, highlighting my goals and assets, even elaborating with stories and anecdotes so she didn't think I was some robotic candidate reading from a script. I was the perfect interviewee— even though I kind of *was* reading from a script, paying less attention to our conversation than to my more immediate task of drilling into her mind. My gaze never left her eyes as we talked. I'd established contact when answering her first question by subtly lighting the tissue of my irises like a firefly's abdomen.

That very sight coupled with the sound of my voice was the hook, and with each subsequent question and answer, a fraction of my consciousness drilled deeper and deeper past her eyes and into her mind. I needed to go deep enough so that, when I planted a certain suggestion, I'd set off a psychosomatic reaction, making a mere wish come true.

Fifteen minutes into the interview, I was deep enough. Her breakfast, only partially digested, wasn't sitting well—so I thought... so *she* thought... The mush wanted out of her. Something in her bowels shifted, making a rumble loud enough for us both to hear. I didn't react when she grimaced; I just kept on answering her question about Jacquelyne Mae's charity work.

There was another rumble and another grimace before she said, "Uh, Miss Mae, pardon me for interrupting, but if you'll excuse me for one second, there's something I must check on."

She stood and walked quickly toward the door, her arms pressed to her sides.

I didn't have a lot of time. Luckily, I didn't require much.

I remained in my chair as I shifted the light around me, creating a thick shell of myself—the appearance of myself—sitting in the chair, stiffly, waiting patiently for Shaw to return. Then I stepped out of the illusion, bending the light surrounding my real body, making it invisible to the camera I'd seen in the ceiling and any others I might have missed.

Some people can easily divide their attention. They can listen to a speech while reading a book on a wildly different subject and retain everything they've seen and heard. I had been trained to do something similar when it came to manipulating electromagnetic radiation. But, as all tricks required physical and mental energy, they were necessarily time-limited. My out-of-body trick would expire in roughly ten minutes.

I took the two drives out of my bag and made for Shaw's computer. I inserted the first one into a USB port. Acquired from one of Bruce's contacts, the drive was first-class spy technology. It worked at lightning speed to download specific information from a computer and any other computers connected to it. Firewalls and all other security measures—at least those used by most in the public sector—were of no consequence. All one had to do was plug it in, sit back, and let it extract. In sixty seconds it was halfway done.

But someone was approaching Shaw's office.

Pruden. *Shit.*

I couldn't stop now, and I couldn't retake my position in the chair.

Pruden entered the office. "Miss Mae? Can I get you anything while you're waiting for Miss Shaw? Coffee? Water?"

Throwing my voice was one trick I'd never learned, surprisingly. I was one of the few ex-Sprytes who wasn't a singer, not even a bad one, and I'd left the fold before I could ever learn. So I'd have to do this the dirty way.

Maintaining invisibility, I got behind Pruden as she cautiously approached the hologram, no doubt wondering why it wasn't moving or responding to her. I put my right hand firmly over her mouth and placed my left arm across her neck tightly enough so she'd be unable to move as I leaned in and whispered a rhyming, alliterative chant. After ten seconds, I released her, letting her collapse on the floor, unconscious and invisible. Singing lessons, no—but I had taken the witch's poetry lessons and mastered them.

I dragged the invisible woman into a corner so she'd be out of the way when I broke and ran, then I rushed to the computer, unplugged the first drive, and inserted the second. More top-notch technology, this one would install malware into the firm's system. When I was long gone it would also leave a message, letting everyone know why Varman had been targeted and warning all others of the same filthy ilk.

Someone else was approaching the door.

Shaw.

And the second drive didn't seem to be working.

Fuck it.

I left the drive where it was and hustled to grab my briefcase and handbag.

Shaw entered the office. "I apologize Miss Mae, but I—" She turned and saw Pruden's slumped body in the corner. "What—?"

I'd released the concentration needed to keep Pruden unseen. I needed it for my next trick.

I got in front of Shaw and dropped my own veil of invisibility. She whipped her gaze from Pruden to me. I could see it in her eyes—she was ready to release a scream that would be heard halfway down the hall. I grabbed the back of her neck with my left hand as I jammed the heel of my right under her jaw. Shaw instinctively shut her eyes, tight.

"Listen carefully," I said before launching into another chant. This one wouldn't render the woman unconscious or invisible. Quite the opposite. It would leave her calm, awake, and alert enough to respond to any questions with some variant of "Nothing is wrong. Please leave me alone."

I felt her body relax. It was working. When her eyes opened, I knew it had worked. I led her to her chair, sat her down comfortably, then retrieved my briefcase and handbag.

The hologram of myself was fading. Shaw's trance would last for just thirty minutes, and the trick would only work if potential visitors didn't progress far enough past her doorway to notice Pruden.

My first instinct was to make myself invisible again, but I needed to conserve energy. I'd spent enough already without even seeing my target. Plus, with my hologram now dissipated, onlookers might wonder where I'd disappeared to.

I nonchalantly walked out of Shaw's office, visible and ready to flash a broad smile at anyone who made eye contact. I'd gone maybe a dozen steps before I had a thought: the ceiling camera in Shaw's office. Surely security had seen me assault Shaw, even if they'd missed me taking out Pruden. *Green mistake.* I quickened my pace.

I always opted for stairs when I could. Elevators were never safe havens, not even temporary ones. Besides, it was easier to fight and deceive one's way through a stairwell. Easier for me, anyway. I located the nearest exit sign and followed it.

I pushed through the door then paused, listening for voices. The stairwell was empty—for the moment. The security guards' office was on the seventh floor. My target was on the thirteenth. I ran up the stairs, appreciating the symbolism as I moved. "Mae" began with the thirteenth letter, and "Jacquelyne Mae" had thirteen letters. All would work to my advantage. The witch had been clever in seasoning her acolytes with all sorts of magicks that relied heavily on the placement of numbers and letters. When I stepped out of the stairwell, I felt I was in the zone. The floor seemed to bounce a little under my feet, as if I were lightly jogging on a resilient running track. And that's how I moved, hustling like an employee running late for a meeting.

There were just as many empty offices on this floor as there had been on ten. The people I did see hardly gave me a second look as I moved. Well, many of the men did, but not because they were suspicious.

My target was in office 13-8, a corner office. As I approached, I heard Varman's voice and that of another man's. Both were equally angry about something.

There was more than one person, and they were both agitated. That wouldn't be a problem. I could probably blind and choke Varman's guest out before—

"Can I help you?"

I paused, shuddering a little before turning in the direction of the woman's voice. I expected a secretary, but the woman wasn't sitting at one of the nearby stations. She was standing just a few feet behind me and wearing a security guard's uniform. Blonde, close-cropped hair; mid 40s; maybe ex-cop or ex-military; not in the best shape, but could probably handle herself well enough. I'd been so focused on Varman's doorway I didn't even realize someone was focusing on me. *Second green mistake*. I couldn't afford a third.

"I, uhm... I have an appointment to meet with Mister Varman."

"How's that? Do you work here?"

"I—" She was going to ask for my firm identification card next, so best not to lie. "No. I used to a long time ago, but I'm interviewing today and I wanted to—"

"*Interviewing*? You don't work here? How are you walking the halls without an escort?" With each question, her voice got louder, drawing more attention. She raised her walkie-talkie, which made onlookers pay even sharper attention.

There was nothing I could say or do to stun her, not with so many eyes on us. Turning invisible was out of the question. So I gambled on option number three.

"Listen," I said, "please don't say anything. I'm his niece, and I was going to surprise him."

The security guard paused.

"We haven't seen each other or even spoken in years," I said, "not since my family lost everything in the typhoon and he sent us some money to get by. Now that I've finished law school, near the top of my class... Well, I didn't want to gamble on whether or not I'd get a job here. I may or may not. I just want to surprise him, let him know how instrumental his money was in getting me to where I am today."

The guard was old enough to be a mother. Whether she was or she wasn't, she undoubtedly had some sympathy for family matters. Cops and military types, the female ones, were like that. And even though I wasn't a musician, I sure knew how to play heartstrings.

"Okay," she said. "Go ahead, but you really should be

escorted. I'll wait out here to walk you back when you're finished."

I clasped my hands in front of my face and nodded. "Thank you." I turned and continued my approach, aware that the security guard's eyes were trained on me the whole time. There was still a chance she was going to call someone on that walkie-talkie. I had to be quick.

Varman and whoever else was in his office were still engaged in a heated discussion. I wasn't sure what they were talking about, and I didn't much care at this point.

I stepped into the doorway. Varman saw me and stopped mid-argument.

"Who the fu—?"

His guest, seated in front of his desk, turned and glared. An older man in a suit, in his 50s, undoubtedly another partner.

"I apologize for interrupting," I said, "but I just had to see you before I left the building—*Uncle*."

Varman straightened a little. He'd gotten the reference. "Uncle" meant one thing to the likes of the security guard and something entirely different to the likes of Varman. It was a code word—a damned, dirty, *disgusting* word that sounded pleasant to the disgusting likes of him.

"May I come in?" I asked.

Varman nodded slowly. He got a better look at me under his office lights. His brow unfurrowed and his grimace twisted like a worm to take the shape of a smile. "Hello..." If worms could talk, they'd sound like this slimeball. He didn't even have enough charm to evoke a snake. It was just as well. It's so *easy* to kill slimy things.

"Prakul," the man in the chair said, "who is this woman? We're not finished discussing the—"

"This is family, I believe," Varman said. "I'm sure you agree family takes precedence over... over what we were discussing. I'll give you a call, Mark. Please close the door behind you."

Mark stood and tossed me a nasty glance as he passed. Age notwithstanding, Varman was clearly the senior partner.

"What can I do for you, *niecey*?"

"I'll tell you what I've told the others before I settled their accounts." I approached deliberately as my eyes drew in light, dimming his office with each step. "There is a ring of pimps in the greater Richmond area, malicious abductors who've taken women—*girls*—and drugged them, kept them high, kept them captive against their will. When arrested, none of these rodents can manage to stay in jail, despite mountains of evidence. They seem to have lawyers on top of lawyers."

Varman was too entranced, too frightened, or too confused to move.

"My research tells me you're one of the ones on top," I said. "A sugar uncle. An *Uncle Sugar*. I got it. I got that twisted joke long ago... A twisted *U.S.A.* A shadowy government fueled by drugs and prostitution. You're a big part of the judicial branch, the supreme court of this shadowy bullshit. But on the surface, in the *light*, you're just a lawyer keeping big-time pimps and pushers out of jail. Apparently, you've been performing all your work for them *pro bono*. I'm not going to bother asking the why of it all. I don't have time to listen to your greasy lies. A slick computer program will tell me all I need to know about *all* the slicksters."

Varman's smile was a distant memory. I saw it in his eyes—he wasn't sure whether to reach for his phone or yell for help. I made sure he did neither by keeping my glowing eyes locked on his as I dropped my handbag and briefcase.

"Who are you?" He spoke in a near-whisper. "*Really* who are you?"

"I'm the one who's going to snuff out your shadow. I'm the one who's going to use you as an example that I can get to *anyone* in your fraudulent government at any time. The injustice system in this area may not care about your kind, for whatever reason, but I do—and I'm going to make your putrid kind extinct."

Varman's hand flinched as he drew in a breath, his mouth opening wider. He was going to scream and reach for his phone. I flared my eyes, unleashing every bit of light stolen from the pitch-black office, shoving everything from my eyes into his. He screamed all right.

That security guard would barge in at any moment. I ran, jumped onto the desk, grabbed a stapler and swiveled just as she entered. I tossed the stapler to my left, enveloping it in crafted light, making it appear as a parrot. Confused, the guard turned her head, keeping her eyes on the distraction as I tossed a cluster of infrared pellets toward the side of her face. She screamed as she fell, hitting her head in just the right way against the door-frame, knocking herself unconscious.

That last bit was luck. I was afraid I'd have to spend a few precious seconds throttling her while whispering poetry into her ear.

I turned back toward Varman. He was writhing on the floor behind his desk, grasping at anything within reach. I'd attempted to fry his optic nerves, probably blinding him for life—not that he had much of it left to live anyway.

I hopped down, turned him on his back, and sat on his sternum, pinning his arms under my knees. I grasped the top of his head with my fingers and placed my thumbs over his eyelids. He kept screaming, but I made sure he heard me.

"I've been saving a special poem for you, vermin."

I applied pressure with my thumbs as I recited it. In the back of my mind, I knew security was rushing toward the office. Someone may've even called the police. A wannabe hero among the office staff had probably gathered up some courage and a broomstick and was heading this way. Didn't matter at this point. My poem was a short one, carefully composed with elements of Varman's name, behaviors, and biography. By the time I reached the sixth line, the struggle had left him. When I reached the eighth, his bones were hollow. At the eleventh, his skin was thin as rice paper. At the twelfth and final line, I twisted my wrists, inserting my thumbs completely, and heard the *hiss*.

I stood up. There were voices behind me, near the doorway. The most prominent one yelled, "Don't move!" I didn't. I didn't even turn to see who'd said it.

But Varman moved. And I'm sure whoever was behind me watched his body float upward and turn face down, its arms and legs splayed, its irradiated skin emitting a glow that inspired hopelessness while the mouth gaped, vomiting a putrid stream of blood, liquefied organs, and stuff even a seasoned crime scene specialist would be too repulsed to try to identify.

Once the body stuck to the ceiling, unable to ascend any further, I turned to see if anyone was still there, still staring. Only two men in suits, possibly senior associates. Both were watching Varman's body, not mine. I could get by them easily, but—hell— why not go out with a little style?

I hopped onto the desk, grabbed a tape dispenser and a ceramic cup full of pens, and tossed them. Flying creatures of light and the mummifying corpse on the ceiling had the two lawyers looking everywhere but at me. I punched and kicked them as I passed, hitting them both in spots sweet enough to ensure they wouldn't get up and follow me anytime soon.

I retrieved my handbag and briefcase and stepped outside the office. Two empty secretarial stations were in front of me. There was a hallway to my left and a hallway to my right. Security guards were coming fast down both of them. They didn't have guns or Tasers, but like the sleeping blonde in the office behind me, they appeared to be either ex-cop or ex-military. Trained.

But trained by mere men, not by a witch.

I tossed my bag and briefcase onto one of the secretary's desks then loosened the cord belt around my waist. My dress went loose as my skin sapped all available light in the vicinity.

I didn't gradually dim the lights this time. I *zapped* them off and made myself appear as an aglow *angel* in the eyes of these men who surely entertained ideas both sexist and sexual.

As expected, they didn't retreat. They pressed on toward me, intending to tackle and do who-the-hell knew what else. *Good—* just as long as they kept their eyes *on* me, particularly on my *pretty* face, which was now the most prominent part of me.

When they were all within ten feet, I pulled back my hair and directed all the light my skin had gathered toward my ears and into my citrine earrings, where the light strengthened before splaying outward.

To say I simply dazzled them wouldn't do me justice—but I meted sufficient justice to the guards. They weren't permanently harmed. They'd wake up in an hour or two. And the outer layers of skin on their faces would probably heal in a couple of weeks.

I retrieved my bags yet again and cut left, toward the stairwell I'd used earlier. Three or four brave-but-foolish souls stepped out of their offices, either to try to understand the source of commotion or to put a stop to it. I put a stop to whatever notions anyone had when I snapped my belt across their faces.

It hadn't been necessary to make the paintings come alive after all.

I barreled through the stairwell door and scrambled up the steps. Not wearing heels had been a wise move. I ascended with relative ease.

The police had undoubtedly arrived by now. They and the rest of the security guards would be in the lobby and on the streets surrounding the building. No one would guess the perpetrator of all this chaos would head to the roof. Who in their right mind would do so?

I didn't stop running until I actually tasted fresh air. I tightened the straps of my briefcase and my handbag, then used my belt to secure them even tighter to my abdomen.

My research had told me the east side of the building would

provide an easier jump. I checked my bags again to ensure they were securely fastened, then I hustled.

I rounded the elevator bank and stopped—*cold*.

It felt as though I'd walked into a freezer naked. I shivered but couldn't take another step as I gazed ahead at Miss Pruden, gazing back at me.

"The police are the least of your worries," she said.

"Who's worried?" I asked. Pruden was unexpected, but she didn't scare me—though my chattering teeth no doubt gave her the contrary impression. "I just took out a menace to society." I tilted my trembling head backward and cast my eyes in the direction of the sun. I stopped shivering. "Guess I'm about to take out another one." I lowered my head and met her eyes.

Pruden approached. "You've interfered with a federal investigation, bitch."

I had goose bumps. My extremities were tingling. I may've been able to move my arms or legs, but I didn't.

"I knew you weren't here to get hired," Pruden continued, "but I knew you were here for some kind of *job*. I tried to research you, tried to figure out who you're with. I initially assumed the IAI—but, no. You're too sophisticated. My best guess? You're one of those Arkangel bitches."

The tingling had subsided but I still didn't move, even as Pruden got within ten feet of me.

"I know you won't tell me," I said, "so I won't bother asking— but whoever you're with, they were moving too slowly. As far as I'm concerned, you're aiding and abetting the enemy."

"Dumb bitch. You have no idea how federal investigations work."

"I know how *my* investigations work," I said. "And I know what it means for one woman to repeatedly call another a 'bitch.' "

We were now no more than five feet from one another, staring eye to eye. There were many different types of Virus-carriers, and among those were many different threat-levels. What kind of medication or drugs did Pruden take? What type of training had she undergone? Did she have a mentor? If so, how vicious and sadistic was she?

I hadn't done the research on her that she'd try to do on me, and I couldn't even guess what cult or clique she'd come from—that ice-light method she used was new to me—but I did know one thing. She was brazen or stupid enough to get this close, look me in the eye, and leave her ears uncovered.

"You have a problem with the word, *bitch*?" Pruden said. "Tough. I call 'em like I see 'em."

"So do I." I dilated my pupils and released a piercing wail to accompany the spillage of light I'd gathered from the sun.

The woman tumbled backward as if hit by a water cannon. I didn't wait to see her try to get to her feet. I ran, gathering speed as I neared the edge of the roof, then leapt off.

While airborne, my specially designed dress and matching jacket reconfigured slightly and combined with my electromagnetic talents to provide enough lift for me to glide to the next building, eleven stories tall. I sprinted across the roof and jumped off the next edge, using the same talents to glide across to the roof of a building roughly the same size. I ran and jumped off the ledge once more, this time letting myself miss the roof and fall a couple stories down, landing relatively unscathed on the fire escape.

Now safely out of sight of the city's flying drones and all the surrounding buildings' cameras, I hustled down the stairs as I monitored my surroundings and modified the appearance of my face, skin tone, and clothes. I retrieved the malodorous perfume from my purse and sprayed it strategically. I then retrieved a bottle of brown and black powder and applied it deftly to my clothes. By the time I hit the ground, Jacquelyne Mae had been put to rest. Walking in her place was a reeking, dirty, wrinkly old bag lady who shuffled along from trashcan to trashcan.

I knew all the drones, cameras, and humans around me would be all too willing to turn a blind eye to what I'd become.

I SMOOTHED the harsh edges and freshened up before meeting Bruce twenty blocks away from the target area. Our rendezvous was a small tea house that sat quietly away from all high-traffic roads. Bruce had undoubtedly cased the place already, but I did the same before going inside.

He was sitting at a two-person table in the back left corner. He'd ordered us the dragon green tea. I could tell by my cup's lack of steam that Bruce had poured it more than ten minutes before I'd arrived. He had either arrived really early or was just unusually impatient today.

I handed him the one thumb drive I had left. He slipped it inside his jacket pocket without looking at it, keeping his eyes on mine as he asked, "Status of target?"

"Terminated." I picked up my cup and sipped. *Yeah* —lukewarm.

He picked up his cup. "Complications?"

"Encountered one carrier. Unknown classification. Possibly HSA, undercover agent."

Bruce furrowed his brow but said nothing. He simply sipped and cast his eyes around the room. Funny. He wasn't hard to read. Hearing mention of the Heartland Security Agency, he probably figured we might be stepping out of our league. Him looking around was a signal that we were possibly someplace we shouldn't be—but in a literal sense it wasn't true. The tea house was empty at this hour. And the owner and his employees were all old friends of his, highly trusted by him when he had been a detective.

"We're fine," I said. "Nothing to worry about."

Bruce looked at me. "The thumb drive?"

"Should contain every email sent and received by everyone at the firm over the last ninety days. When we get back you'll need to search for keywords and then cross-reference any names on your old list."

Bruce nodded. "The other one?"

"Not sure it worked. But I left it in, just in case. I got surprised and had to get out."

"And leave them your thumb print," Bruce said. "I told you you should start wearing gloves."

I chuckled. "Yeah. Wearing gloves to an interview makes sense."

"They can run your prints. The right person... the *wrong* people will be able to trace—"

"My original identity is dead, Bruce. Let them try."

"Your new HSA friend will try, you better believe it." He sipped and cast his eyes around again, this time with good reason. Two patrons had walked in. A male and a female, early college age, both wearing dull expressions. I doubted they were any kind of threat, but maybe Bruce had other ideas. He wouldn't take his eyes off them.

"Let's head back," I said. "I want you to get started on that information. And I need to plan for tomorrow."

We left cash on the table and walked toward the front exit. Both of us glanced at the college kids on the way out. The female glanced back, but the male paid us no attention whatsoever. They wouldn't be a problem.

Outside, Bruce looked around and said in a lowered voice, "The medications are in the car. You want to take it?"

"Where are you going?"

"Might be a good idea for us to split up"—he again looked over his shoulders—"I know you've been careful and all. But I don't like this HSA business."

I didn't like the fact I hadn't been able to detect Pruden as a carrier when we shared the elevator. She was a variant—that much was clear. But what would the HSA want with her? Why would they plant *her* there instead of a clean agent? Hell, it was probably for the same reason I waltzed in there so easily. The woman was more handsome than undeniably beautiful, but there was no denying she was attractive in all the right ways. Whether that was a trick of light and makeup or just actual fact didn't matter. People would listen when she wanted to tell them something; people would open doors for her, pull out chairs for her... let her open files, let her easily pull out secrets.

"The HSA is probably investigating this so-called shadow government, too," I said. "So what? That's what they're supposed to be doing. But their intentions don't matter. They're so tangled up in their own red tape, they're tripping over it. That's the inevitable nature of bureaucracy. That's why I work solo."

Bruce cocked his head.

"You know what I mean," I said.

The two college kids came out of the tea house. We both watched as they walked. The girl again glanced in our direction —twice—while the boy seemed to pay no mind. I felt less easy about them now, less easy about *her*. If I'd learned anything over the past few years, it was that teenage girls on the cusp of adulthood could be big trouble. But the two simply got into their car and drove away. It was time we did the same.

"We're *not* splitting up," I said.

Bruce shrugged. "Okay, Betty. Have it your way."

I followed him to the alley where he had parked the town car, out of the sight of drones and cameras. I looked around while Bruce ensured the car hadn't been tampered with. We then got in and drove off, keeping off the main roads as much as possible.

"You'd be wise to be wary of the HSA," Bruce said after we'd gone a couple of blocks. "You know my old department worked with them on a couple of cases? Some of those guys, they're not all that they seem."

"Whatever they are," I said. "I've seen worse." *Much* worse—even before I contracted the sexually transmitted Virus.

A burning for social justice had flared up in me at a young age after seeing the way my father treated my stepmother, someone to whom I logically should have felt little connection and even less loyalty. But maybe those early flames were too bright. I made it through college without a clear idea of what I wanted to do with myself. I'd spent my energy studying and arguing and only found relief from the constant stress by learning yoga and massage therapy. Straight-up meditation was a no-go for me. At the end of four years, I'd gained knowledge and weight, but I'd no better sense of place, no wisdom. I only felt bloated: fat and over-stuffed on liberal arts.

Going to law school was the fashionable path for wayward college grads, a route to job security if not happiness. My first semester there was rough, but during the second I met a teenage girl, a very charming girl who despite her young age was acquainted with some of my female classmates. She provided them, and eventually me, with supplements that increased awareness and made it easier to focus. Those damned, sweet pills made me sensitive in so many ways...

That's how I ended up sleeping with the wrong guy.

In my third year, when I first exhibited violent symptoms of the White Fire Virus, I again met the girl. She was strolling the hospital halls. At first, I thought it was just chance, but later—much too late—I figured it was by design. She told me she had other supplements—some deep, *deep* black market stuff—that could help me cope with my new condition and eventually master it. Not only would my life not be ruined, but it could change for the better. I could finish law school, feeling as healthy as before, and as laser-focused as before. But there was one catch. The girl wanted me to engage in extracurricular studies with her and her circle of friends twice a week, and then four times a week after I graduated.

The way the supplements made me feel, I was happy to agree to anything. I was just as happy to land a job practicing corporate law after graduating in the upper tier of my class. But, out of all lawyers, the recession was most ruthless to the corporate ones. I held the job for the same amount of time most people stay on their honeymoon. At the charming girl's behest, I began spending more time with her and her associates—the Ladies of the Light, as she sometimes referred to us en masse, and quite ironically, as much of that time it seemed as if my head was in a fog. I don't clearly remember the initiation process. Hell, I don't even remember fully agreeing to become part of some magickal cult. Nonetheless, I ended up as a Spryte, a living weapon and instrument for the witch Carmilla, the so-called Girl of Many Charms.

Unlike the other women who'd totally fallen under her spell, though, I was never fully in line. And after one particularly ugly incident, I broke free. The witch had trained me well enough so that I could cover my tracks and stay hidden. But I couldn't confine myself to a cave for the rest of my life. I needed a decent place to stay. I'd have to pay rent, and I'd have to eat. I couldn't apply for a job in my profession, not even as a paralegal or a document reviewer. That would've made it too easy for Carmilla to find me. So I resorted to using the talents I'd long ago acquired in order to put myself through college: giving therapeutic massages to anyone willing to pay. I was certified as a massage therapist, but few seemed to care so long as I untangled the knots in their muscles and rubbed their stress away.

And yet the amount I earned as a run-of-the-mill CMT just wasn't cutting it. There's no shortage of stressed out folks during a recession, but many were extremely careful about how they spent their money. Still, I had customers, and I liked what I did. I liked it even more when I discovered finishing off with a happy ending led to much bigger tips. Twisting my technique so that the massage was sensuous from beginning to end allowed me to double my price and increase my clientele.

It was all highly illegal but, as Bruce constantly joked, it was also more honest than what most lawyers did. I'd met him during this time in my life. He was the lead detective in charge of breaking up a sex trafficking ring in the Richmond area. For some reason or another, one of the pimps he'd rounded up had my number stored in their smartphone. Maybe I had unwittingly given one of them a massage, or maybe one of them had found my number on a "good rubs" site and had saved it with the intention of recruiting me. Whatever—Bruce tracked me down by himself. He confronted me and interrogated me on the spot, gazing into my sepia eyes...

He slid into the palms of my hands—*beautifully*. I helped the detective see the reasons behind my way of life. Soon after, he turned in his badge, telling his superiors he was going to work in the private sector. With a wry smile he told them he was going to be a private dick. Together we found a safe place off the radar of both our former overseers, then I helped him continue his investigation. It soon became *my* investigation as I dug deeper and deeper into the dirt, and the detective who'd been repurposed into my valet helped me take out the garbage.

Now the HSA might have gotten involved. The Heartland Security Agency's mission was to protect America's children and preserve traditional families. More than any other government agency, they were tasked with strengthening the country's moral fiber, a key factor in keeping America stronger than any other country. They should've known about this ring and broken it up long before I ever even heard of it.

We stayed silent during the drive, but the expression on Bruce's face and his occasional sighs made it clear he was preoccupied with the thought that the HSA was aware of our vigilante escapades and might confront us. The man was an open book.

We took a shortcut through yet another long alley as I said, "Nothing to worry about—"

"The *fuck*?" Bruce slammed on the brakes as he shouted.

A Lamborghini had sped out in front of us and blocked our way.

It was time to worry.

"Back—" I began, but the former detective didn't need any prompt from me. He'd already put it in reverse and floored it. He stopped at another intersection, no doubt wondering whether to turn right or left. He had only a split second to ponder as we saw a Ferrari speeding from the left, a Jaguar from the right, and a Porsche coming up fast from the rear.

"Shit!" He switched gears and pushed the accelerator, speeding forward. But the Lamborghini had turned into the alley and was heading straight for us. An Aston Martin was right behind it.

Bruce slowed the car; he was beginning to panic. An open book... He was contemplating a game of chicken.

"Stop the car," I said.

"What? I—"

"*Stop* the car," I repeated. "Put it in park."

He did. The other cars stopped as well.

I'd immediately recognized the vehicles' style. All were sleek, brightly colored, armor-plated, and engineered to go much faster than the models available on the public market. I had a sudden and brief regret for the loss of my Corvette Stingray. But even that wouldn't have gotten me out of this.

I opened my door. "Stay in the car—"

"Are you crazy!" Bruce interrupted. "What're you—"

"*Stay* in the car," I repeated. "They're five of them. One in each vehicle. They're too narrow to bother with passengers, and they'll leave you alone if you don't try to antagonize them. So just stay in; I'll draw them away. When I've got them occupied, you get out and run."

"I—"

"Don't question it. Not now." I got out of the car. "Make your way back home—*smartly*. I'll explain everything then, if you want to hear it... and if I make it back."

"What? You—"

I slammed the door, ignoring whatever Bruce was yelling about. I walked toward the rear of the town car and kept on going, casual but careful about my surroundings, ready to defend myself. Trying to break for it would've been stupid. The ladies could run as fast as tigers if need be.

The driver's side doors of the luxury cars all opened at once. The ladies stepped out and moved forward like fashion models on a video shoot. Their appearance matched their movements. All were well over six feet tall. I was so focused on their slinking bodies, I didn't notice whether they'd even closed the car doors behind them.

As they approached, I turned in a circle, watching them, sizing them up, until they stopped, placing me at the center of their circle. The five of them stood equidistant from each other and from me... like five points in a pentagram.

Shit.

I didn't recognize them, but it was clear the witch had trained these Sprytes well.

"Barbara," the bob-cut brunette said, "I believe this is she. Confirm?"

"I confirm," replied the one with the wavy red hair. "What are your eyes telling you, Brittany?"

"My nose is telling me more," said the one with the hime cut. "What do you think, Beverly?"

"No question the skunk is intimate with this one," the pixie-cut blonde answered. "I believe we've found our woman, Bellissa."

"A happy reunion," said the dark chick with the finger wave, "and yet she looks so sad. You'd think she'd be relieved for the opportunity to get clean again, right Bethany?"

"Some of the dirty don't know they're dirty," the brunette said, "until they're clean enough to smell the flowers."

I chuckled away my nervousness as I looked at each of them in turn. "What, no *Brunhilda* among you? Carmilla must be losing her sense of twisted humor."

"You're the one who's lost, Beatrice," Beverly said.

"The Mistress sent us to retrieve you," Bethany said.

"I figured," I said. "I also figured Carmilla knew I wanted nothing more to do with her. Thought I made that clear when I stuck my Stingray into that hideous statue of her." I turned as I spoke, trying to keep my eyes on each of them. "The moniker's 'Betty' now, by the way. I really have declared my independence."

"And yet," Brittany said, "you're using magick that does not belong to you."

"I'm using what I learned while she used me," I said, "while she used *all* of us as bait." I shook my head. "You dumb, beautiful, zombies... The witch tied us up in strings of lies and dipped our souls into another dimension, not giving a damn about us. I got out in time, but you... Your bodies ended up distorted, stretched. You can't think a thought without her approving it first. And all for what? What do you get out of it?"

Their answers ran counterclockwise.

"We were all born again."

"Attaining wisdom."

"Understanding."

"*Power*."

"And the promise of eternal life."

"*Bullshit*," I said. "Carmilla destroys pieces of your soul every time she uses you. You're all too far gone to understand anything. She keeps the real power for *herself*. If her prophecy is even partially true, if there is a life waiting for us—for you—after all this, it will only be as her eternal slaves. I'd rather devote myself to this world, *freeing* slaves. I don't belong to her, and if you weren't under her noxious spell, you'd realize you shouldn't either."

"Beatrice—"

"*Stop* calling me that." They were trying to exercise a form of magick known colloquially as Verbalism. Word Magick. All five of the women had names or, more likely, *pseudonyms* that began with the letter B and had three syllables. One simple purpose in adopting such names was to disorient their targets. Another was to acquire, share, and redouble their power. The action of introducing themselves out loud and accepting their given name in turn sealed a bond, making the ladies more powerful as a whole. And if I, at the center of their circle, accepted a name that fell into that same category as theirs, they'd gain a nearly unbreakable psychological hold over me. I'd used a similar form of magick with Bruce. I changed my original name to click with his, but his name had only one syllable. I had allowed him *some* agency to think and act for himself.

In unison, the five women took two steps closer, tightening the circle. These Sprytes were good, but I'd learned more than a few tricks during my brief tenure as one of them. I spread my fingers and tensed my forearms. They undoubtedly heard the crackle of static as loudly as I. They had the additional treat of seeing the tangles of multihued light pulse under my skin.

"We're not here to fight you, Beatrice," Bethany said.

"Just to warn you," Barbara said.

"And make you an offer," Bellissa said.

Bethany said, "Return to the fold by noon tomorrow, and all will be forgiven."

"Return by dawn," Brittany said, "and all will be forgotten."

"But miss either deadline," Beverly said, "and the Mistress will be forced to send Hunters next time instead of Gatherers."

I glanced over at the town car. The driver's door was open. Bruce was gone.

"And where exactly would I go?" I asked.

"Any of the Mistress's properties," Barbara said. "Once you step foot on one, she'll know you're there."

"But if you're not in place when time is up—"

"Your soul will end up out of time."

"In *no* place."

"What will have been the point of your life then?"

They each backed up four steps before turning their backs to me and slinking back toward their cars. I didn't move until they'd driven away.

The witch had found me, and she could find me again. But I had a choice. Unlike the ladies speeding away, I still had free will, and a conscience.

BY THE TIME I returned home, Bruce was already hard at work. He was so focused on his screen, he only noticed I was a few feet behind him when I coughed.

He stood and turned, reaching for his gun. He was more jittery than usual—but I didn't flinch. When he recognized me, he took a deep breath and put his hands on my shoulders. I kept mine at my side.

"Did they hurt you?" he asked.

"Not physically," I said. "They just gave me a few things to think about. They... They're—" Something was wrong with my tongue.

Bruce tightened his grip as he looked into my eyes and shook his head. "I know it's not something you're ready to talk about. That's fine. But I have something we should discuss." He let go and nodded toward his laptop. "I haven't gotten through all of it, or even most of it, but look at what I found..." He sat. "Several emails between a high-ranking HSA official and Varman."

I leaned over his shoulder. I no longer felt tongue-tied.

"I'd think an HSA official would be more careful about covering his tracks," I said. "Varman, too, for that matter."

"Maybe someone was just overconfident about the promises of attorney-client privilege."

I snorted. "Yeah. What were they discussing?"

"Politics. Religion. And something about a voluptuous fifteen-year-old redheaded girl that the HSA official wanted to *buy* in order to, and I'm quoting, add to his collection."

"Looks like I have my next target."

Bruce smiled. "Thought you'd say that. So get this..." He punched keys, moving through screens at a rapid pace. "The guy is getting married tomorrow."

"Where?"

"Here." A picture of a beautiful vineyard appeared on his screen. "It's up in Loudoun County."

"Time?"

"Eleven a.m."

Eleven in the morning... *One* and *one* next to each other, in mourning... I immediately began planning my strategy. I had my name and outfit already picked out. I just wondered if I should slit the guy's throat when he started to say "I do," or when his misguided trollop did. Or maybe when they kissed?

"It's at least a two-hour drive," Bruce said. "We'll have to wake up around three or so."

"I'm heading up tonight," I said. "It'll be smarter and more efficient for me to scout the territory well before dawn. In the meantime, I want to know everything I can about this guy. Everything about him, his would-be bride, the guest list, the vineyard, and the surrounding terrain."

"*Really*? All that before you leave?"

"Contact some of your friends. Call in some favors. Do whatever. I'll pack my own clothes and accessories. Have me what you can before I leave and be ready to send me the rest by five a.m."

I hoped I was doing a good job of covering my anxiety. I didn't want to be anywhere near Richmond by dawn. And I didn't want to think about the Sprytes. Only by concentrating fully on my next target could I put them out of my mind.

"Is any of this going to be a problem?" I asked.

He stared at me, the corners of his mouth turning downward.

"Have you ever considered you might be on the wrong track?" he asked. "Or... or just going too fast down the rails? Or—"

"Or maybe *off* the rails?" I said. "Was that what you were about to say?"

He gaped at me for a moment then shook his head. "No. None of this will be a problem."

IT WOULD BE my first time crashing a wedding, but there wasn't too much I needed to plan. It was outdoors. Getting in would be easy. Getting out, almost as easy.

I'd worn a tan brown war-dress, an outfit designed by one of Carmilla's acolytes and inspired by some characters in her favorite book of narrative poetry. The outfit was reinforced in all the right areas to help one fend off bullets, fire, and blades. A woman who really knew how to wear it would look fantastic while dancing, fighting, or simply standing still—but the belt was what really completed the package. It was a fashion accessory that could hold some pretty nice accessories. Mine holstered a pair of nine-inch blades.

The winery had three buildings, all converted barns, and one of them had been prettied up enough to serve as living quarters. Rows and rows of vines surrounded them; heavily forested hills were not much farther out. Making myself invisible would be a snap in the daylight, and switching to camouflage among the trellised vines would be no harder than two snaps. Escaping into the woods would be child's play.

Presently I was camouflaged and positioned comfortably in a

tree with a good view. Bruce had sent most of the remaining research I'd requested to my smartphone by dawn. The HSA rat was marrying some tart nearly half his age. Bruce had trouble getting me much info on her background, and he had even more trouble getting details on the guest list. Best he could tell me was that most attendees would be friends of the groom and coworkers of the bride.

I digested pieces of information as I watched the organizers set up. I could've moved in closer but I preferred to stay put, doing my best to keep the branches and leaves around me still while using any and all optical tricks to study everything.

I hadn't slept a wink all night. Instead, I'd cased the grounds, measured distances, and planned attack methods and escape routes—anything to keep my mind off the Sprytes' deadline and everything to ensure no one snuck up on me in the dark.

I'd stayed jazzed through dawn and sunrise, watching the set-up like a vulture, mildly curious about the large and irregularly shaped wedding gifts stacked on top of and around one table. I couldn't see through the wrapping, but I didn't spend much energy trying. The guests, as they trickled in, commanded most of my attention.

Rather than suits or dresses, all were wrapped from head to toe in fashionably arranged scarves featuring a variety of patterns —combinations of black, white, and gray. Only their eyes, their manicured hands, and their stylish shoes were visible. I made a few reasonable guesses, but it was near impossible to tell who was a man and who was a woman. None wore heels or loafers or any other footwear that leaned toward one gender; unisex plat-form shoes or boots all around. I'd tried x-raying in the area of the chest and crotches of a few, but much like the gifts' wrapping paper, something about the composition of the fabric prevented me from seeing through.

Was mummy chic the latest fashion for weddings? Or was this couple just ahead of the curve? Regardless, the colors and styles seemed more appropriate for a bizarre funeral than a fun wedding. Maybe the HSA agent was more of a twisted sicko than Bruce's intel had let on.

Speak of the devil…

The groom exited from one of the former barns and sauntered toward the gathering, walking quite properly in straight lines and making right-angle turns. A slender man wearing some kind of full-body black suit that covered everything but his eyes, mouth, and maybe nostrils. It wasn't quite skin-tight, but the outfit was close-fitting enough to dispel any questions about gender. What was it? Leather? Spandex? Rubber? Of course my sight couldn't penetrate the material—but I was sure one of my blades could.

And here was the bride, all decked out in white. A small, thin girl wearing another full-body suit that only let eyes and mouth greet fresh air.

If nothing else, I admired the wedding planner. After this was over, I'd have to look her up, maybe recruit her and have her design me some new outfits. She and Bruce could be the beginning of me building my own little fashionable team of vigilantes.

The bride and groom took their positions, and the officiant—an oddly proportioned figure wrapped in the most colorful scarves—raised his or her hands majestically, commanding all attention and silencing all tongues. Even when this master or mistress of ceremonies began to speak, its gender was not apparent. *No matter.* That fool wasn't a target.

I manipulated the light around my body—transitioning from camo to invisibility—as I levitated down from my branch. I took care that my footfalls were softer than a cat's as I crisscrossed through the rows of vines and made my way to the house. It took no great effort to scale the side. From the roof, I could easily jump and glide, felling the groom with one swipe, if not decapitating him outright. I'd resolved to do it right after he and the bride kissed, when they'd undoubtedly have to pull off those ridiculous masks.

I was tense. *Ready*. Then the preacher called for the ring.

There was no best man. There were six pallbearers.

Enwrapped in black scarves, they exited one of the buildings and walked a dividing line between the guests toward the bride and groom. They carried a crystal coffin. A sleeping teenage girl lay inside. A chubby redhead—naked, bruised, blemished, freckled, and scarred. Some of her wounds had healed badly; others seemed freshly made, suppurating, slowly healing, scabbing over...

What the hell was all this?

Bruce had mentioned the HSA agent had wanted to buy a redheaded girl. Was this her? Was this wedding-funeral also some sort of auction?

Whatever—the idea behind it all was clearly disgusting. It was time to inject a dose of beautiful chaos.

Still invisible, I leapt and glided at a strategic angle with a double-edged blade in both hands. I was seconds away from cutting away the groom's mask with one and slitting his throat with the other.

The officiant raised his or her hands erratically as something enwrapped and wringed my wrists, forcing me to release my grip, before jerking my entire body off course. I crashed into the gift table.

Stunned, I relinquished my invisibility as I tried to stand.

I couldn't.

I couldn't get to my feet.

The blow hadn't been that hard; I'd suffered worse. The trestle table hadn't even cracked. Neither had any of my bones. The problem was the gifts—their *ribbons*. Some of them had untied from their packages and tied themselves around my arms and legs. They felt like silk against my skin until I shifted or tried to move; then they felt as strong and as sharp as steel. The harder I tried to free myself, the tighter they felt, the *deeper* they cut.

I was now a gift, and I immediately knew for whom.

The officiant, the bride, and the groom loomed over me.

The bride was first. She put her fingers to her neck, parted the seams, and pulled her mask off.

The girl... that *damned* girl from the tea house.

The groom was next. At this point, it shouldn't have been as much of a shock as my voice made it seem, but since my body was trapped, my emotions were getting away from me.

"*Bruce*? What—? You—You, *shit*! What the fuck are you doing?"

He sighed. "I'm sorry, Bet. But they... they..."

"We met up with him during your escapade yesterday," the college girl said. "We made a deal, and we kept our eyes on him to make sure he kept it."

"What *deal*?" I threw the question at Bruce.

"Delivering you to me," the officiant said. "*Alive*. At least, for the moment."

I knew the voice, knew it all too well. It had sounded deeper when she was conducting—or *pretending* to conduct—the ceremony. But now the witch sounded like her regular old ugly self.

She unwrapped the scarves that covered her hair and much of her face. I sat bound, trapped, looking up at the girl whose skin tone gave the impression of a corroded penny.

"You went through a lot of trouble," I said. "Are you that desperate, that *scared* of losing something that doesn't belong to you?"

"No trouble at all," Carmilla said. "Everything important involves ritual and ceremony. And all my Sprytes are valuable, too valuable to be loose, floating purposeless in this world."

"*Witch*, do you have any idea what I've been doing? You should have put your resources at work to help me."

"I know exactly what you've been doing. From day one. I let

you go on your merry way until it was necessary to call you back. Now, I've *called*."

"Appearances are deceptive, witch. You still don't have me. You'll *never* have me."

Carmilla smiled and lowered her face closer to mine. " 'Betty,' is it?" She shook her head and *tsked*. "Really poor choice of a nom de plume. You're up against a goddess of gambling, you know. I've yet to lose a bet."

"Maybe," I said. "But all the women you've tricked and kept under your control have lost plenty."

"You mean their names in exchange for wine from the Vine of Life?"

"I mean giving away their bodies, minds, and souls in exchange for a deranged madwoman's bid for Godhood."

Carmilla shrugged as she straightened. "The clothing of thin skins, rotting flesh, and limited minds won't withstand the environment of the new universe."

"And free will? What about that?"

She laughed without making a detectible sound. "I guaranteed you eternal life, *Bet*. But now... Now you want to die having accomplished nothing meaningful."

"I've killed pimps, child enslavers, molesters—some of the ugliest creatures on the planet."

"Uglier ones are coming," Carmilla said. "You were re-made to serve one purpose. The Sprytes have one lofty duty: To help save a *beautiful* child."

The pallbearers brought the crystal coffin into view. I hated, hated, *hated* myself for thinking it—but the girl inside was in no way pretty, never mind beautiful.

"It's really simple," Carmilla said. "We help save this girl, she in turn helps save the chosen for the Hereafter. As I've tried to teach you, The End is very, very near."

I struggled again with the ribbons and bled for it. The Carmilla I knew was not this talented, nowhere near this powerful. Something had happened since I'd left her fold, maybe something that had to do with this redhead, or maybe some of these nameless, faceless *things* around me. They may've been exercising some sort of influence over the environment. That had to be it. I understood the manipulation of light, not the manipulation of fabric, nor other manipulations... I cast a glance at Bruce, who may as well have been a statue.

"The shadow government," I said, refocusing on the witch. "You're involved somehow. *Why*?"

She smirked. "All governments, whether in shadow or light, will fall. They are of no consequence. My involvement with them or lack thereof is of no consequence. I simply make deals, temporary arrangements with whomever I need to achieve the ultimate. And you"—she nodded at me—"I'm giving you a choice. An ultimate choice. You can decide whether you want to be of any consequence."

"Really?" I tried my best to smirk back at her. "Do you really need me?"

"Despite your transgressions, I'm willing to welcome you back, with no hard feelings."

I struggled with the steel ribbons, again drawing blood.

"But I can't just give you a written test," Carmilla said. "Or an oral one. Poor student that you were, you'd undoubtedly fail. And I want to give you a *fighting* chance."

The ribbons around my arms and legs loosened as some anonymous wedding guests pushed forward two packages, both more than eight feet tall with silver wrapping and golden bows.

I stood, although I didn't know whether it was by my own willpower or that of Carmilla's. She stepped backward, beckoning me forward with her index fingers. I wasn't sure of myself. And I wasn't sure whether the guests had unwrapped the packages or if they had swung open on their own to reveal two tall, fashionable figures: A blonde and a raven-haired brunette, both adorned in war-dresses much prettier than mine.

The blonde predominated in red while the brunette favored blue. They had belts, but no weapons were attached. They stepped out of the boxes like dolls come to life and flanked Carmilla. I had a fleeting impression of the two being Carmilla's accessories. They were the blades in the witch's belt.

"Bet," Carmilla said, "I like to introduce you to Blink"—she pointed a thumb at the blonde, then the brunette—"and Blank. I refer to them and some of the other ladies you've met recently as Killer B's." She laughed another silent laugh, quite appropriate for a humorless joke.

These two were like the women I'd met yesterday, but there was something more to them. Tresses of the blonde's hair obscured her right eye, and the brunette's eyes were so deep in shadow, even out in the midday sunlight, that I couldn't even determine the color of her irises.

When facing off against another Virus-carrier, it was more important to be aware of an opponent's eyes rather than the hands or feet. As I tried to study the eyes of the two ladies, the blonde smiled, and the brunette frowned.

I grimaced. I hadn't come here expecting a real fight. I'd already spent so much energy staying in hiding and sneaking up on a false target. Even at full strength, I wasn't sure I could engage these two and win. But there was no other way out, no way to escape without shedding even more blood.

I dove for blondie, who seemed the softer of the two.

She twirled and dipped, as if led by an unseen dancing partner—but she was in control enough to grab my ankle as I passed.

Blink flung me toward her very visible partner—Blank—who kicked me in the neck. Her foot felt like a brick of ice.

Down on my hands and knees, I was surprised my neck wasn't broken as I turned my head to see blondie's blurred foot nearing my face.

I flattened and rolled away from the reach of both women before scrambling to my feet and dashing for the gift table.

I went for the smaller packages, tossing them, enfolding them in waves of light, making them appear as fiery, flying demons.

It was such an automatic attack method for me that I didn't pause to consider how it might work on those who were equally talented or even more talented.

Blink and Blank dodged and twirled, again as if dancing, moving closer all the while, until they were close enough to dart in on me with sweeping motions.

One went high, the other low. I hopped and bent backward, flattening myself on the table as one of them smoothly ducked under it while the other glided over me.

It was funny how many thoughts a person can have in a split second; they really do slice by at light speed. I congratulated myself on the quick maneuvering and mentally laughed when they failed to connect while at the same time wondering what really made these two living dolls so special as I—

Hands clasped my wrists and ankles.

From beneath the table, Blink had my feet. At my head, Blank held my wrists. Together they pulled, stretching me.

My bones popped, even—*especially*—in parts where there were no joints. The women were doing more than just pulling; they were running a current through me. It was the opposite of a massage. I could imagine-hear-*feel* hairline fractures forming in my bones throughout my body. They were going to break me and rip me wide open.

I looked toward the sky, squinted, and concentrated like a desperate worshipper of Ra.

My skin tightened. My muscles tensed. I ran some currents of my own.

I felt my nerves snap and crackle just a few decibels lower than the shrieks both ladies made when they let me go.

I rolled off the table and quickly scanned my surroundings

for the least-resistant path for escaping. The guests were most sparsely clustered at ten o' clock; that's where I darted.

As I neared bodies, I shouted rhythmically, like a cheerleader, trying to encourage the people to move their damn selves out of my way. But they didn't hear me. *I* didn't hear me. My voice box may as well have been an icebox, my tongue a tiny frozen waterfall.

Fuck it—I was prepared to barrel on through the crowd of would-be mummies. A block of ice at the back my knee made me tumble instead.

Blank had caught up and landed a well-placed kick. To replace the shout of pain that somehow wouldn't come, I kicked at her knee in turn. She *blanked* out before I could connect, and the other one *blinked* into sight at my right to kick me in the side of my head.

I rolled with it. Dizzy, I managed to get to my feet. I lunged in the direction of the blonde, only to see her pop out of sight and feel the other one pop in behind me when she kicked me in the lower back.

I wouldn't go down again—I *couldn't.*

I did my best to keep my balance while turning and swinging. Of course she was gone, and I fell to the ground.

But maybe luck—some *beautiful* luck—was on my side. I saw one of my blades within reach. I stretched and grasped it. It was like having an appendage reattached, an appendage that worked effectively and instinctively.

I stood again, if not steadily then at least sure enough to keep my face far away from the ground as I maneuvered, slashing and slicing at everything near me. But the two nearest me were Blink and Blank, who kept blanking out and blinking into sight before I could so much as cut a thread from their clothing, let alone penetrate a layer of skin.

Then one of them appeared inches in front of me, her right hand in an ice-cold vice grip around my throat.

Raven hair—*Blank*. Even at this close range, I could barely make out her irises.

It was then that I realized she and her partner, their names, their methods, and their appearances were all part of some ritual, a very poetic ritual well beyond my understanding.

Everything is ritual... ceremony...

She smiled as if reading my thought. I made a move to plunge my knife into her abdomen. She opened her mouth and *hissed*, spraying a cold perfumed mist all over my face before letting me go.

The fragrant spittle warmed quickly and burned like acid, washing away my makeup, letting the sun play havoc with my face, and distorting my senses of sight and sound.

As I stumbled, trying to fight back against the loss of direction, the loss of my place in this wide chaos, the ceremony progressed as the surrounding crowd sang a song. To my ears it sounded like a turgid dirge that made numerous connections between love and blood, marriage and war. They sang as they moved, keeping me and my two *elusives* forever encircled. And from somewhere both beyond and amid it all, I heard Carmilla, taunting me with crystal-clear words as Blink and Blank assaulted me with hands and feet I couldn't see coming.

"Your tricks are corrupt. *Rough*. Not sublime. Not beautiful. *Ugly*—like you. You truly don't know what you're doing, or why."

The witch was right. I couldn't win. I couldn't escape. I couldn't even speak. I just continued to move, twirling, whirling, sweeping, and windmilling my arms in attempts to smack, slap, cut, and chop my two enemies, my two dancing partners... partners who cut up my dress, slapped away the tatters, and chipped away at my makeup, my skin, my flesh...

They wouldn't take my mind. They *couldn't*.

But they had drawn me into a pattern, and my movements were just giving it further details. I was losing it—my body, my consciousness...

My last coherent thought was of Bruce, my trusted valet. Yesterday, he'd procured the medications I'd taken this morning. There was no question about from whom he'd really gotten them. There was no question that I couldn't trust anyone any more. Now, all was Blink and Blank—kicks, punches, and tosses —until it all went *black*.

My eyes were opened by a song.

This one was joyous, far more cheerful than the one that had accompanied my thrashing. It had the tone and words of a true wedding song; the refrain was "Always." The same crowd of enwrapped wedding guests sang it. They were fanned out before me, like tangible spirits, solidified ghosts. And I again was entangled, this time in vines, hanging from a trellis at the edge of the vineyard.

Carmilla, Blink, and Blank stood mere feet in front of me. Each held one hand behind their backs and the other upraised, grasping a crystal goblet half full of what appeared to be white wine.

"Congratulations," the witch said. "I've decided to welcome you back."

The three of them clinked then sipped from their glasses.

"Wh-What..." My larynx and tongue were as unsteady as my eyelids. "What... what is all this? What's happening?"

"Reparation," Carmilla said. "You were a wreck before I found you and tried to repair you, beautify you. But you got lost, and I found you again—"

Something quickened within me, sharpening my senses and my tongue.

"Li-like a rusty instrument," I said, "or a broken robot... That's how you see women, *all* women who aren't under your complete control. You were never any better than the pimps I've executed.

All you want is pretty, plastic-skinned tools, all of them working to create something they'll never truly share."

What I'd said had been honest from the heart, but the words weren't completely mine, nor was the energy that spurred the outburst. I cast a glance to my left and spotted the crystal coffin and the comatose girl inside. Was she—that *ugly* girl—reaching out through me? Using me to cry for help?

Whatever the explanation, there was nothing I could do about it; the green vines entangling me seemed stronger than steel. And for her part, Carmilla was oblivious to any connection between me and the girl. The witch kept her eyes on me as she spoke.

"You keep trying to break free," she said, "but you have always been nothing more than a damaged doll, a puppet with limp limbs and fraying strings, not fit to be released from her packaging yet. You had a philosophy, but it didn't make complete sense. You had a course of action, but the path was too dark and had no end in sight. I tried to teach you the underlying lessons of New Creation, but you saw flaws." She chuckled. "Sister, there was *never* any flaw in my magick; there were only flaws in your being. But you have wisdom enough to understand that you can't be allowed to exist. It's necessary for me to kill my *ugliest* creations."

She and her companions revealed their hidden hands; each held a long blade. Blink and Blank clutched those I'd brought with me. Carmilla's, with its jewel-encrusted hilt, was clearly ceremonial but no less sharp.

I had no words. And even if she had inspired me before, the girl in the casket was now as lifeless as she looked. All of my hope lay in the coffin with her.

This, *all* of this, wasn't just the gathering of a lost soul. This had been a demonstration for the guests—the nameless and faceless of Carmilla's nextworld government, bidden to sing without understanding the words. They were witnessing what happened to traitors because there was so much at stake in the grotesque game of war that Carmilla was playing.

"Beauty has been cheapened in our society," the witch said. "And so has death. But don't worry. I'll make yours mean something."

Carmilla zipped her blade across my throat; Blink and Blank mimicked in rapid succession. In unison, they raised their glasses. I forced my eyes to stay open as I felt my last breaths leave me. I could only maintain long enough to see the three swirl their glasses, hold them up to the sunlight, then take generous sips.

The only words I heard before my senses blurred were "Welcome back into the fold."

ABOUT THE AUTHOR

Harambee K. Grey-Sun writes under the broad umbrella of speculative fiction. He integrates elements of fantasy, horror, noir, black humor, and science fiction into his work and spins dark, surreal, mysterious, grotesque, at times challenging, and often blasphemous tales. Many of his stories can be categorized into one or more of the following subgenres: speculative thriller, urban fantasy, metaphysical fantasy, superhero, occult/supernatural, slipstream, and–*of course*–weird fiction. His Dark Metaphysical Fantasy series *Eve of Light* examines the dark nature of God and what it really means to be human.

For more information:

Click Here for Author's Website
www.harambeegreysun.com

ABOUT THE SERIES

Eve of Light is a Dark Metaphysical Fantasy series chronicling the surreal events leading up to the Apocalypse—the Death of God. The setting is a contemporary, alternate Earth on the verge of a cataclysm that will warp space, time, and minds. The main narrative of those plotting and battling to save humanity is told in the *Eve of Light* series of novels. The short stories and novellas are simply flashes on the fringe—episodes told from the perspective of everyday men and women living in a world turned weird.

The Core Novels
BloodLight: The Apocalypse of Robert Goldner
Broken Angels *(Eve of Light * Book I)*
Divinities, Entangled *(Eve of Light * Book II)*

Stories on the Fringe
FoolKillers
The Lark
Heaven's Gun
Knotty & Ice
Rogue Beauty
Deviant-Hunter's Sabbath

ALSO BY HARAMBEE K. GREY-SUN

Standalone Stories

Beholder

Love Among the Ultramoderns

The *EVE OF LIGHT* Series

<u>The Novels</u>

BloodLight: The Apocalypse of Robert Goldner (*Prequel*)

Broken Angels (*Book I*)

Divinities, Entangled (*Book II*)